miss conduct

A CURVY GIRL AGE GAP INSTALOVE ROMANCE

MAN ON A MISSION SERIES: BOOK ONE

LIA PRESTON

LUNARIA PRESS, INC.

First Edition

Print ISBN: 978-1-7388946-4-2

Cover: Lunaria Cover Design
Editing: Eyes on Your Story

Published in Canada by Lunaria Press, Inc.

one

PAIGE

"No, I can't do that." I shook my head at Elle as she led me to the bar, glancing at the older man at the opposite end.

I'd made the critical error of mentioning he was hot a few minutes before. And he *was*. Tall, lean, broad-shouldered with dark graying temples and ice-blue eyes that made me shiver when I'd caught him glancing my way. He was wearing a thin, v-neck, cashmere sweater with the sleeves pushed up to his elbows. His lean but muscular forearms were on display. He may have been older, too old—for me, anyhow—but damn, he was sexy.

Elle spun on her heels, and I crashed into her. She popped a hand on her hip. "You're going to talk to him. I didn't make the trek to Seattle to help you set up a new, more exciting life for you to turn into the same old wallflower on day one. Not happening, Paige. If you won't go to him, I'll bring him to you."

I shook my head at her. That sounded even more

embarrassing than chancing a hello, because knowing her, she'd make a big deal out of it. She was *that* friend, after all. As much as I loved her outgoing ways and all the adventures we'd been on because of them, this pushed me way out of my comfort zone.

"He's a little old, don't you think?"

She shrugged at me. "It's like wine. Men only get better with age."

I wouldn't know anything about that.

Not. One. Thing.

Because at twenty-four years old, I hadn't sampled any vintage of the 'wine' she spoke of. Okay, I may have had a sip or two. In the form of a bit of fondling and foreplay on occasion while I tested the waters. But something was always missing for me to want to take it to the next level. My virginity, in the traditional sense, was intact.

Elle was the opposite. A dose or two of her moxie and I'd save myself from becoming a forty-year-old virgin. Never mind the fact that at the rate I was going, I'd be greeting my casket hymen intact. I sighed. Maybe she was right. It was about time I stepped outside of my comfort zone.

We sat down on two empty bar stools before she leaned over. "Okay, so are we doing this the hard way or the easy way?"

I wasn't too sure which was which. Both of her suggested ways seemed 'hard' to me. Glancing down the bar in his direction, I watched him as he swirled the little straw in his highball glass before discarding it on a napkin and taking a sip. His Adam's apple bobbed as he swallowed the drink. The stubble on his face was trim and neat.

I looked back at Elle. "The easy way?"

She perked up. "Perfect. Let's get you a drink and then you get your cute little butt over there."

'Cute little butt.'

Cute, maybe. It depends on who's looking. Little, not a chance. I had more than enough junk in my trunk. If it was an actual car trunk, it would overflow and have a bungee cord strapping it closed. Too bad my breasts didn't get the memo.

My heart thudded in my chest. Was I up for this? He was handsome for sure, but what could I offer a man like him? I was fresh out of college and starting my first proper job working at Velocity, one of the premier marketing agencies in the country, as a social media marketer.

Elle poked me in the arm. "Look, the seat beside him is free now. Go. It's your chance." With that said, she just about pushed me off my stool. Before I knew it, I was on my feet, putting one foot in front of the other, with a lump in my throat. I glanced at the bar door.

The desire to bypass him and leave overcame me. I looked back at Elle, who waved me on. She'd never let me live it down if I ran out of there. Besides, why was I concerning myself with what I could offer him? I was only going to sit next to him and talk to him.

Maybe.

If he was interested in talking to me at all.

My dress fabric snagged on the stool as I attempted to sit on it, and my foot slipped off the rung, causing the stool to wobble. Two hands wrapped around the small of my waist, steadying me.

Smooth Paige, smooth.

I straightened myself on the stool. "Thanks," I choked out in his general direction, my cheeks burning, unable to look his way.

He let out a laugh. "No problem."

There, I talked to him. That had to be enough, right?

The bartender approached me. "What can I get you?"

I opened my mouth to reply, "I—"

"She'll have water," he said. His voice was low but soothing. Like honey over gravel.

The bartender turned away, and I looked over at Mr. Silver Fox with a question on my lips.

"You almost missed the stool. I think you can take a break, don't you?" He winked a silvery eye at me.

"I'm not drunk," I blurted out but even I could hear that I sounded like an indignant child. I wanted to shrink up and disappear where I sat.

"Could've fooled me. So, you're just uncoordinated?"

"My dress got caught on the stool. Well, it's not my dress. It's my friend's dress. She lent it to me because we wear the same size and there's nothing in my wardrobe that she considers 'club worthy'. And I don't but—" But what? Why was I telling him all of this?

He scanned my dress. "It does look hazardous."

I looked down at myself. It contoured my hourglass shape, but the blinding silver sequins flashing under the bar lights were the only things 'hazardous' about it. I felt like a human disco ball. Or was he referring to how tight it was? At least it had a zipper down the front because fitting into it without one would have been a nightmare. Still, his comment confused me. "What do you mean?"

He pulled his phone from his pocket and tapped on it before setting it on the bar and looking over at me. "I should have said *you* look hazardous in it. You're bound to give someone a heart attack. It's a good look for you. Is your friend here? I should thank her on behalf of all men."

No way.

I needed to get my hearing checked because he didn't say what I thought he did, did he? Was he—was he flirting with me? "Umm, thanks."

The bartender set down the water.

Cashmere sweater man put his hand up, signaling for the bartender to stay. "Order a drink. What would you like?"

I laughed. "Oh, I'm allowed one now?"

He nodded.

"Ah, sure, vodka and cranberry?"

"Put it on my tab," he said to the bartender before swiveling on his stool to rest his elbow on the bar.

"You know, you're pretty bossy for a stranger," I said.

He raised his eyebrows and smirked. "I just like to look out for pretty girls at bars. Is that a crime?"

"No, I suppose not."

"I haven't seen you here before."

"You're a regular, then?"

"Well, not really, no."

It seemed odd to me. Why would a man of his age and apparent stature come to a place like this? He didn't fit in. The crowd was young.

Oh.

Maybe that was his thing. Young and naïve women. He was pretty forward with his compliments, after all. The confidence he exuded only added to his already attractive exterior. But I hoped I hadn't just sat down next to a predator.

What if the protective thing was an act? Designed to get women to trust him, only to take advantage of them later. I'd watched a documentary about a con artist that did that. I looked at the Rolex on his wrist. What if it wasn't real? Or worse yet, it was, and he'd been conning young women into giving him every dime they had to afford it?

Slow down, Paige.

I needed to cool it with true crime documentaries.

"Do you have somewhere to be?"

"No, why?"

"You were looking at my watch."

I laughed, thankful that he couldn't hear my thoughts. "Nope, I have all night."

He smiled, revealing a perfect set of white teeth. His eyes crinkled some as he did, but it only made him even more handsome. A smile looked at home on his face. If he was a con man, he was a happy one. "In that case, I'm Rhys." He reached a hand out to me.

I took it. "Paige." He rubbed the back of my hand with his thumb and those icy eyes locked on mine, sending a wave of heat cascading through me.

"Nice to meet you, Paige."

My stomach danced. I don't think I'd ever enjoyed the sound of my name more than I did coming from his lips. It was a sin and a prayer all rolled into one.

My throat dried up as he let go of my hand.

"You said you're here with a friend?"

I looked down the bar to where I'd left Elle. She was gone. I scanned the dance floor, finding her. "She's over there."

He glanced at her. I regretted pointing her out. She looked seductive out there dancing and was drawing a crowd. "I'm guessing since you had to borrow an outfit, that this isn't just a regular Friday night for you two. Are you celebrating something?"

The bartender returned with my drink, and I thanked him before I took a sip. "Yes. She made the trip from Portland to Seattle with me to help me get settled in before I start my new job."

"That was nice of her. Where are you work—"

Just then, a man in a suit tapped Rhys on the shoulder. He turned and greeted him. "Sorry, Paige, I'm here for a meeting. You'll stick around, I hope. Because when I'm done, I'd like to continue this chat."

He stood and placed his hand on the small of my back. "If not, I hope Seattle and your new job treat you well."

"Thank you."

He left with the other man, and I watched as they went through a door, which I assume led to an office of some sort. It made a lot more sense that a man like him would be here on business. I should have asked him what kind of business he was in. Or anything at all. I realized while I'd been buzzing from the entire experience, I hadn't asked him anything about himself.

So, yeah, I screwed up.

Elle must have been keeping her eye on us because only moments later she was at the bar seated in his spot. "How did it go? Did you get his number?"

I shook my head. "Good, but no, I didn't. He called my dress hazardous."

"To his health maybe, you look bomb in it."

"That's close to what he said." She looked down at the bar and her jaw dropped before she looked at me out of the corner of her eye, hers twinkling. "Look what he left behind."

His phone.

"I'll bring it to him." I picked up his phone, slid off the stool, and started toward the door he had gone through. Elle was hot on my heels. She slipped her arm through mine, steering me toward the women's washroom. "What are you doing? He's in there." I pointed to the door.

"And he'll get it back, Paige, but not until we give him a little something to remember you by."

She yanked me into the big stall and locked the door behind us before pulling at my zipper. "You need to show more cleavage."

"Are you kidding me?" The top curves of my breasts were in plain view, with my nipples barely covered by the balconette bra I was wearing. "What for?"

"We're going to make him regret not asking for your number."

She slid her finger across the lock screen, opening the camera.

I shook my head and laughed. "You're crazy. And how did you do that without his password?"

"Now you're the one kidding me. You own an iPhone, Paige. Did you not know that you could take pictures without unlocking them?"

"No, I've never needed to."

"Well, you can. Pose."

I reached out to take the phone from her and she pulled it back. "I should just bring him his phone back."

"And you will. Relax. We're just going to have a little fun first."

I stared at her, contemplating it.

"Never mind, it's okay." She held the phone out to me. "It was a dumb idea. I'm sorry for being pushy. You went to talk to him. Which I know is out of your comfort zone. I'd call that a success."

I chewed at my lip. His smile flashed in my mind. Why did he have to be so hot? I wondered how he would react to seeing pictures of me on his phone. He hadn't hidden the fact that I was attractive to him. And I was more attracted to him than anyone I'd ever met before.

It was the poise, the confidence, and the protectiveness. I'd ruled out him being a con artist. Maybe if not for the interruption, he would have asked me for my number. But it was silly for me to have to wait for him to ask me for mine. We had his phone. I could just give it to him, couldn't I? Moving to Seattle was all about taking charge of my life.

I smiled at Elle. "Let's do this."

"No way! Are you serious?"

"Yeah, why not?"

She did a little shimmy before holding the phone up.

I unzipped the dress a little more, letting the sides fall away from my bra. If I was going to do this, I was going all in.

I posed, and she snapped a picture. I spun around and hiked up my skirt just enough to let the bottom of my ass cheeks peek out of the dress and looked over my shoulder.

"Fuck, I wish my ass looked like yours." She leaned back to get a better angle and snapped the picture.

"There's nothing wrong with your ass."

"Maybe not, but it's non-existent compared to yours. Turn to the side and arch your back."

I did as she said, and we went through a few more poses. Finishing our photoshoot with a video of me giving him my phone number and blowing him a kiss.

"Damn, girl. You're going to send him into cardiac arrest."

"Let's hope they resuscitate him, and he calls me."

"Oh, he's one-hundred percent calling you after this."

It was crazy. We had to be insane to do what we'd just done. My heart raced thinking about him seeing parts of me that almost no one had ever seen. But somehow, I was okay with it. And that was a first.

I felt like he would be the one man that could touch me in the way I'd always craved. The gentle hesitant caresses of past ex-boyfriends just didn't hit right. I wanted a man's touch. Rough, self-assured, and commanding. I might not have had any clue what I was doing, but I didn't want the same in a partner. Rhys seemed like the kind that could do some guiding.

We left the bathroom, and I hurried to the door with his phone clenched in my hand. I didn't want to lose my nerve. The security guard stepped in my way.

I pointed past him. "Rhys, the guy in the meeting, left his phone at the bar. I just wanted to return it to him before I go."

The security guard nodded and took the phone from me, slipping into the room without a word. I turned to Elle when I realized what I'd just done. "Okay, let's go. I don't want to be here when he gets out."

"Why?"

I grabbed her hand. "I don't know. Let's just go now, okay? I'm hungry."

She furrowed her brow. "Are you okay?"

"Yeah, I'm fine." But it was a lie. I pulled her to the door and took a deep breath once outside. The pavement glistened from recent rainfall. I took in the lights of the city before me. I felt like a changed woman, and I had Elle, a chance encounter with a wobbly bar stool, and Rhys to thank for that.

two

RHYS

When the meeting ended, the bouncer handed me my phone. "Where'd you get this?"

"A girl in a glittery dress said she needed to give it back to you before she left.

"She left? How long ago?"

He shrugged. "Five minutes ago? Not even."

Good. Maybe I still had a chance if I hurried. I darted around him, a little peeved that he didn't let her say goodbye to me.

You're assuming she tried to.

Maybe she wasn't interested in me that way. Maybe she was just another young thing that saw the Rolex and figured she could get a free drink or two.

No.

Not Paige.

I crossed the busy bar, heading for the doors. There was an innocence about her. The way her cheeks flushed, and her eyes widened when I complimented her. It couldn't have been an act. It brought out every protective instinct I had in an instant. She was the most stunning and genuine woman I'd met in, well, forever.

Bursting through the door, I looked left, then right. She was nowhere to be seen. Just then I caught a flash of her sequin dress as she climbed into a cab across the street.

Darting across the busy road like I was in a game of frogger, I dashed for the cab. Slamming my fist on the trunk as it pulled away from the curb. Her head spun to reveal her sweet face peeking out the rear window.

She turned and said something to the driver before she opened her door, and stepped out. Her friend poked her blonde head out of the cab behind her with a shit-eating grin on her face. Why do I get the distinct feeling it wasn't Paige's idea to approach me earlier?

"Rhys? Is something wrong?"

I moved closer to her. "I think you know what's wrong."

Her eyes were like saucers. "I'm sorry—your phone—I shouldn't have."

What was she talking about?

"My phone is irrelevant, Paige. I'm talking about the fact that you were running off before we got the chance to get to know each other better."

"But I left you a—"

"Forget it." I didn't want excuses. She was all that I wanted, and the thought of losing track of her didn't sit well with me. We'd only just met, but I couldn't stomp down the nagging voice in my mind that insisted she was mine. That if ever there was a time to take a risk, it was while standing there in the street with the most stunning woman I'd ever met.

I pulled Paige to me. Her friend let out a loud gasp. "You left without me being able to do this."

I grabbed her by the chin, tipped her head up, and pressed a kiss to her full lips. I kept it friendly at first. A peck. But when I felt her body melt into mine, I knew it was okay to deepen it.

Kissing her after one conversation was a risk, but when I set my sights on something, I was determined to get my way. It was true for business, but less so in my personal life because Paige was the first and only woman I'd desired in a very long time.

Once I broke our kiss, she was breathless. Her body was still leaning into me for support.

Her friend tossed something from the cab onto the pavement then turned to the driver and said go. She slammed the door of the cab shut before rolling down the window and popping her head out as it pulled away from the curb. "I have your house keys. Text me when you're home. Misbehave yourself!"

Paige's head whipped around. "Elle!" She yelled, but it was too late. Her friend had deserted her.

With me.

I moved around Paige to retrieve what I realized was a purse from the pavement. That was a ballsy move, abandoning her friend as she had.

I handed Paige her bag. "You've got quite the friend there."

She wrapped her arms around her, tucking her clutch under her arm. "Yeah, that was a first."

"Why would she have done that?"

She rubbed her upper arms and shrugged.

"Are you cold?"

She shook her head no, but it didn't matter. I slipped my jacket off and set it over her shoulders. She must've been cold, her dress was skimpy, and it was fall. Which in Washington state meant enough humidity to chill you to the bone if the temperature dropped.

"Thanks. She just wants to see me take more chances."

"With strange men?"

She cocked her head at me. "Just how strange are you?"

I smirked. "Are you asking to be cheeky? Or do you want to know, little girl?"

She gasped.

I laughed. "No stranger than you can handle. I promise." And it was true. I'd only known her for a short time, but there wasn't even the tiniest chance that I'd cross any line she didn't want me to. "Are you hungry?"

"I could eat." She gave me a shy smile that made me want to kiss her again, but I didn't want to overwhelm her. "Come along. My car is just around the corner, but there's a truck that serves amazing food that's parked there around this time of night to catch club traffic." I looked at my watch. It was only a little past midnight. "Shouldn't be too busy yet, but once the clubs close, you can forget about it."

I took her hand in mine, leading her down the street. Making certain my long stride wasn't too much for her to keep up with. I may have just met her, but I wanted her by my side. Tonight. And depending on how she felt about things we'd see about tomorrow. Hell, I was ready to clear the week for her if she asked me to.

She was quiet as we walked. I pointed out things to her here and there, playing tour guide in my home city. She seemed interested but rarely commented.

I stepped down off the curb after pointing out our most famous landmark. She craned her neck, to look at the Space Needle.

Then she pulled out her phone and snapped a few

pictures. "I wish I had my camera with me." She gestured at the tower. "It's smaller than I thought it would be."

I winked at her and led her across the street. "Let's hope that's the only thing you'll be saying that about tonight."

She snorted out a laugh, and a bright smile overtook her face. "I wouldn't worry about that. I have no frame for comparison."

We reached the opposite curb, and I turned to face her. Was she saying what I thought she was? "Are you a virgin?"

She bit her lower lip and nodded. "I don't tell people that so soon. And even when I wait, it doesn't go over well. So, if you've changed your mind about this. Or *us*. I understand."

Changed my mind?

No.

It did change my expectations of the evening ahead, though.

She pulled her hand from mine. "I know that expression. It's okay, you can spare me the speech."

"No. You don't know, Paige. Have you ever dated a *man* before?"

"Of your age? Well, no."

"Not just of my age, baby girl, but a decisive man who knows what he wants and goes for it. I'm not some little boy looking for a cheap thrill. I've had a fucking lifetime of them."

The smile on her face told me she didn't need any further convincing.

I reached out for her hand. "Are you ready for the world's greatest hot dog?"

She placed her hand in mine. "Is that another attempt at innuendo?"

"We'll soon find out."

three

PAIGE

"How am I supposed to fit this in my mouth?"

Rhys laughed. "With some determination. Consider it a training session."

I sucked in a breath. Heat flaring in my core. I'd spent many of my twenty-four years wondering if I'd ever want someone the way I was supposed to. The way others seemed to, but I never had. Feeling my brain was—broken.

The city lights, combined with the dark abyss of the Pacific Ocean visible in the distance made the night feel like it was brimming with magic. Like amazing things could happen at any moment. My eyes met with Rhys's. Amazing things were already *happening*. I'd finally found him. The one capable of making me want it all.

I wished I had my camera with me to capture every moment. There was a time when almost all I did was view the world around me through a lens. I'd often felt a disconnect from much of what was going on around me, and for years my camera made that easier. But for the first time in forever, I felt grounded just staring into his eyes. It was unexpected. Unreal. And I was ready for all of it.

I set down the hot dog. It may or may not have been the world's greatest tasting, I hadn't even tried it to find out, but it was large enough that it might've been record-breaking. Then again, there was probably a hot dog large enough to fill a city block somewhere in this bizarre world.

"Giving up so soon?"

I took a sip of my drink. "No. I'll tackle it in a minute. I'm just curious about something."

"Go on," he said before taking a bite of bratwurst.

"I know it's not appropriate to ask. But I've already over-shared. I'm wondering how—uh—"

He swallowed and frowned. "Forty-six, Paige. I'm forty-six years old. Is that what you wanted to know?"

I nodded my head. Wow, he was older than I thought. Not as old as my father at fifty-two, but pretty close. My sister had already challenged the status quo with her forty-two-year-old fiancé, Andre. And she was a couple of years older than I was. Still, Rhys looked incredible. He wasn't how I would have imagined a man his age looking, but I'd never been an expert judge. "How are you not married already?"

"I was. Years ago."

"Divorced then?"

"No, I wish. At least then, she'd still be alive. Even if she wasn't with me anymore, that would have made me far happier than losing her the way I did."

My heart shattered for him in an instant. "I'm sorry."

"It was a long time ago, Paige. But you'll understand one day if you don't already. When people leave too soon, there's something so unsettling about the injustice of it all that you never quite get over it."

"Did you have any children?"

He shook his head. "No. We tried. That's how we found out about her uterine cancer. I just wish we'd discovered it before it had metastasized." He paused and ran a hand through his dark hair. "Sorry, this is a terrible first date conversation."

"You can continue. I understand if you don't want to, though. As you said, it's the first date."

"There's not much more to the story than what I've told you. It all happened very fast. Too fast, in fact, but it was a long time ago."

I nodded. There was something about him that made me want to know everything about him. Good, bad, and everything in between. I picked up my hot dog and took my first bite. It was a better idea than trying to make more small talk. I was failing on that front.

The food was juicy, spicy, and as close to fine dining as a hot dog bought on the side of the road could get. And I'd grown up on fine dining thanks to my chef turned hotelier father. I chewed, swallowed, and wiped my face with a napkin. "This is incredible."

Rhys smiled. His eyes were an even more chilling blue in the streetlights. If it was even appropriate to call them blue. "I'm glad you like it. Back to age. How old are you?"

"Twenty-four." He was almost twice my age. I must have been crazy for sitting there entertaining our connection.

"Hmm."

"What, no retort on that one? Does it bother you? My age?"

"You're younger than I thought," he said with a half-smile.

I guess neither of us was an expert judge of age.

"Does it... change things for you?"

He shook his head with a laugh. "Please stop asking me that. Did I not make myself clear earlier?"

"You did, but—"

"But, *nothing*. Eat your hot dog before it gets cold."

My stomach fluttered at his commanding tone, and I squirmed in my seat a little. Was this normal? I'd never been turned on by someone telling me to eat before. We'd only just met and I was ready to throw myself at him. I wished I had the nerve to act on it.

We ate in silence for a few minutes.

But it was long enough for my flutters of arousal to be deadened by anxiety.

Had I questioned his intentions one time too many?

He finished his hot dog. "It changes a few things, Paige. If you want the truth. You're young. I'm not. You haven't experienced men to the fullest yet. I've experienced enough to know what I want from a woman. What I want to do *with* a woman. But do you?"

I took a sip of my lemonade, washing down my bite. "That's not fair. You've asked me not to question your interest. Why do you get to question mine? Did you ever think that maybe I have such little experience because nothing felt right before? I refuse to see that as a flaw in my character, and if you do—"

He cut me off. "Does it, now?"

"Does what now?"

"Does this feel right to you? *Us.*"

"Yes."

It shouldn't have. At least, not so soon. And not with a man twice my age. But with Rhys. Everything aligned in an instant.

"Then, finish up. I have one more thing I want to show you."

four

RHYS

"This is the most disgusting or the most interesting thing I've ever seen. I can't decide." Paige stood in the alley, scanning the countless colorful wads of gum adhered to the brick walls.

I'd stopped at a corner store for a couple of packs of gum on the way, the kind a child might chew. Pink for her and blue for me. I wanted her to experience it while she was still a tourist in this city.

"This is your Seattle initiation."

She smiled. "You're giving me the full Seattle experience in one night. What am I going to do tomorrow?"

I wrapped my arm around her waist, pulling her close. "I can think of a few things." Leaning forward, her breath hitched. Her lips parted, and her eyes fell closed. A gesture that was so vulnerable it made my cock twitch. But that would have to wait. Our first kiss was a surprise. I wanted the second to be unforgettable. I popped a piece of gum in her mouth. "Chew."

Her eyes shot open. I'd never tire of shocking this woman. She had the most captivating stunned expression I'd ever seen.

"Under any other circumstances, if a guy seemed like he was about to kiss me and put a piece of gum in my mouth instead, I'd be offended."

I smirked at her. "You'll be doing more with that mouth than just chewing if you keep giving me lip."

She swallowed hard with a gulp.

"Did you just swallow your gum?"

"Yes, and I'm going to choke to death if you keep saying stuff like that when I have something in my mouth."

"Ah—" That one was *too* easy. She reached out as I handed her another cube of pink bubblegum before I put a piece of the blue in my mouth. We chewed them until they were soft.

"Where should I stick it?" She pulled the wad from her mouth.

This woman was killing me.

"It's a wall covered in gum, babe. You make the rules."

"I feel weird about it. It's like vandalism."

"City officials might agree with you there, but people have been doing this since before you were born. No one's gone to jail yet, as far as I know. Stick away."

She walked up to the wall and stuck her gum on a bare corner of brick. I put mine next to hers, overlapping it. "There, now you're stuck with me."

She laughed, while she dug through her bag, pulled out a little bottle of sanitizer, and squeezed some in her palm before offering it to me. We coated our hands in it. "It's like I knew some handsome man would come along and force me to do disgusting things with him tonight."

I stalked closer to her. "Stick with me and you'll learn

that I'm into far filthier things than this." I pulled her further down the alley, away from the germy attraction, and backed her against a clean wall. Okay, maybe clean wasn't the right word for an alley, but it was better than where we were before.

"If you think sticking gum to the wall is the dirtiest thing you can do in an alley with me. You'd be wrong."

"And what do you mean by that?" She coaxed me on. I could see the desire building in her eyes, even in the dim light.

"How much experience do you have with men?"

I wanted to bend the rules with her but not break her.

"Some, but I think what you're asking is if I'm ready for more. Yes, Rhys, I'm ready."

That was all I needed to hear. The consent to have my first true taste of her. I planted a needy kiss on her lips. Her arms wrapped around my neck, holding me close. She parted her lips, and I deepened the kiss, but I still wanted more.

I needed more.

More than a taste.

More than a simple touch.

I wanted everything with Paige. Everything she would share with me. With her breasts pressed up against my chest, I wished I'd taken her home instead of into an alley. Thoughts of her naked in my bed and ready to be taken by me flooded my mind.

As I slipped a hand up her thigh, I could feel the heat emanating from her pussy, inviting me closer. My fingers ran over the thin fabric, eager to explore the almost untouched treasure that lay beneath.

I broke the kiss. "Fuck, I want you, Paige. I want to feel you from the inside."

She moaned against my lips, and I snuck my fingers beneath the hem of her panties, her body shivered, as I did. She was wet.

So, fucking wet.

So ready.

Like a peach, round, ripe, and heavy with juice, begging to be plucked from the tree and devoured. I found her clit and started working at it. Her soft moans echoed off the brick walls of the alley, amplifying my need for her.

"Rhys. Rhys, I—"

I backed off her clit, not wanting it to end yet. Not when there was still so much more of her to be explored. By my hand, and maybe, if I was lucky, my cock too. I slipped two fingers into her, and she gasped at the penetration. I couldn't get over how tight she was.

Curling my fingers to massage her g-spot as my thumb found its way to her clit, her moans grew louder and more frequent. I was certain that any passersby on the street could hear her. It was tempting to smother her mouth with more kisses, but greed won out. The desire to hear every bit of pleasure she felt from my touch entranced me. I didn't give a fuck about anyone or anything else at that moment. I wanted to make her come.

No.

I *needed* to make her come.

"You're the most gorgeous, amazing, and sexy woman I've ever met."

My cock was rock hard in my pants, begging for release. But I wouldn't even contemplate that until she had hers.

Her moans turned to whimpers. "Come for me, pretty girl. Give Daddy what he wants." She was so close I could feel it. Her body was alive with desire, squirming and vibrating from my touch. She grew tense for a moment and sucked in a sharp breath. Her thighs clamped around my hand as she broke, throwing her head forward and crying out into the nape of my neck. Riding the waves of pleasure that overcame her.

Like a fucking teenage boy, I almost came in my pants at the same time.

I reached for my zipper. It wasn't how I wanted things to go down for her to lose her virginity in an alley. But I'd make it up to her later. I needed her that fucking bad.

But something wasn't right. Her body trembled in my arms.

I pulled back to look at her face. She was pale, too pale.

"Are you okay?"

"Uh, I, yeah…"

"Paige, don't lie to me."

"It's just… I've never… That's never happened before."

"You've never orgasmed before?"

"No, I have, just not like that. Not with anyone else."

I smiled, wrapping my arms around her as she rested her head on my chest. "You'll get used to it. I'll take you home now. That's more than enough for one night." I kissed the top of her head.

A few minutes later, her trembling subsided enough for her to walk.

I felt overcome by the obvious. Dumbfounded because I'd found the woman that could make me feel again.

I was more stuck on Paige in one night than a million pieces of gum ever could be to a wall.

five

RHYS

"Mr. Lockwood, Martin is on line two for you." My assistant, Naomi, told me over the phone.

I leaned back in my leather executive chair, thanked her, and switched lines.

"Marty, good to hear from you."

"Rhys, you prick. Your pitch the other night was so fantastic you've secured all nine of the marketing management accounts for Westwood holdings."

"Did you think I couldn't change their mind? You lost the bet, so you're paying this weekend." Martin and I had both been in the marketing game together for a couple of decades. We'd weathered the storm of young upstarts and the tides of an ever-changing scene together.

"I thought for sure this time you'd fail."

"I keep telling you not to bet against me. It only makes it more of a guarantee that I'll push to win."

"Fuck, man, this friendship is getting expensive."

I laughed. "You meant to say your gambling habit is getting expensive." I looked at the time on my computer. It was almost nine in the morning. "I have to swing by the new hire orientation in five. Get the contracts drawn up and schedule a meeting for this afternoon before he changes his mind."

"You got it, boss."

I rounded the corner to the boardroom a few minutes past nine. I pushed the door open and stood, arms folded, at the back of the room in front of the doors.

The presentation had already started. All I saw were the back of their heads. Some of them were scribbling notes. Why? I wasn't sure. They were learning useless information about the company. Information that they should have already known about us. But I didn't give a damn what they knew about our history. I cared only about what they could offer our future. The door behind me flew open, slamming me in the back before I could dodge it.

A woman gasped. "Oh no, I'm so sorry." The entire room turned to see what the commotion was about, and I turned to see who the source of the interruption was.

Who didn't have the common fucking sense not to make a scene while sneaking into a boardroom late?

I froze.

"Paige?" I said aloud before I could catch myself. We'd exchanged numbers and a few texts, but she had her friend in town for the weekend, so I told her to focus on her because we would have all the time in the world after she left.

Apparently, I was wrong.

She met my gaze and let out an audible exhale, as though my presence had sucked every ounce of breath from her lungs. Her eyes were wide like a deer about to be in a head-on collision. What was I saying? It was a literal collision. I straightened my back and turned away from her.

Fuck me.

It was a disaster.

What was she doing in my boardroom?

Rhys, you idiot, someone in your company had hired her.

Did I need to start monitoring all of my department's new hires to make sure that I didn't finger them in alleyways the weekend before they started working for me?

No, of course not.

She edged her way around me to an empty chair at the back of the room. I waved my hand at the trainer to continue the orientation.

It wasn't like I made a habit out of doing what we'd done together. Paige was special, one date was all it took for me to want her. It wasn't just her sweet yet sexy looks. She was bright, quirky, and fun. I'd never been as fascinated by a woman as I was by her.

And that's why her showing up was a fucking disaster.

I watched her empty her bag on the table. Pens, highlighters, a leather day planner, and a notebook cluttered the tabletop. To say she was over-prepared was an understatement for sure. She leaned forward in the chair to watch the presentation. The arch in her back drew my eyes to her full ass. The one I remembered filling out a sequin dress so well it should have been criminal.

No, what was fucking criminal was me staring at her how I was. I turned my attention back to the presentation. I'd spent all weekend fantasizing about the various ways I could plunge my cock into Paige. Dreaming up different ways to make her first time memorable.

I should have been counting my blessings that none of that had happened. That I'd only explored her with my hand. And that I wouldn't be battling even more intimate details of her body daily.

I glanced at her as she peeked over her shoulder at me, her expression pinched.

Fuck me.

Her concerned look made me long to clear the boardroom of the others. So I could grab her and say, 'You have nothing to worry about, baby girl'.

But that would have been a lie. She had plenty to worry about, or at least, I did.

Because fighting off my desire for her wasn't going to be easy.

I wasn't used to losing once I set my sights on something, or in this case, someone.

And from the moment I'd laid eyes on her I wanted her to be mine.

She wasn't kidding when she said her usual wardrobe was different. She wore a white button-up blouse with long sleeves and a loose skirt. Was she going to work or bible study? Not even that shirt could hide her perfectly sized pert breasts, though. I flashed back to the cleavage she was rocking the other night. Sure. I couldn't see it anymore, but I *knew* it was there. There was just enough to bury my face in and not want to come up for air for days. I ripped my gaze away from hers again. We'd been staring at each other for a beat too long.

This wouldn't work.

"Mr. Lockwood, is there anything you'd like to add?"

Yeah, I'd like to pull Paige to my office, lock the door, tell her she's fired, and bend her over my desk and fuck her.

I shook my head. "No, you go on. I'll be back soon."

Slipping out of the boardroom, I strode toward my office. I couldn't get away from Paige fast enough.

Naomi watched me, her brows furrowed, while I zoomed past her desk. It was unlike me to return so soon. I hadn't even stuck around long enough to evaluate the abilities of the recruits during the activities.

But I couldn't handle it.

Not with *Paige* there.

Once in my office, I sat in my chair, leaned back, and shut my eyes.

If I was looking to escape her, being alone with my thoughts wasn't the way to do it. A flash of her dark brown hair cascading down her back, and her bright smile, struck me. Followed by the way she'd swirled the straw in her drink while she thought about her responses.

Enough.

I snapped forward in my chair, picked up the phone, and paged Naomi.

"Did Martin get that meeting with Westwood?"

"He did, yes. It's at one."

"Good. I'm going to head out now."

"It's only 9:30 a.m."

Like I needed her to read the time for me.

"I know. I have a few preparations to make." *And a new hire to avoid.*

"All right, Mr. Lockwood. Will you be back this afternoon?"

"Maybe. I don't know. It depends on how long the meeting runs. I'll let you know."

No, I wouldn't be back, not if I could help it. I needed

some time to center myself. Enough time to put the other night into perspective and reframe Paige in my mind.

She was too young.

She was my employee.

And she was *fucking gorgeous.*

Damn it.

A woman hadn't caught my eye like her in decades, if ever. Her curves were perfection. She was plump and ripe for the picking, and if the taste I'd had of her the other night was any sign, she was every bit as delicious as she looked.

I grabbed my briefcase and rushed out of the office to the garage and slid into the driver's seat of my Tesla.

I had to get control of myself.

My phone buzzed.

PAIGE

I'm sorry, I didn't know.

Of course, she didn't, neither of us did. As incredible as she was, as long as she was my employee, we both needed to resist. It was against the company policy. In the early days, I'd established a no fraternization policy after I had an issue with a couple of my employees who went through a tough breakup.

It resulted in the one moving on to a competitor's firm and taking a couple of our bigger clients with them out of spite. Though I suspected it still happened, I didn't want to invite chaos back into Velocity once again by authorizing it. It wasn't worth destroying my company or her career.

I know you didn't. I'm sorry too, but I need to ask you not to text me again.

Have a nice first day.

I found her contact and deleted it along with our text history. As much as I knew it was the right choice, it felt wrong. Every bit of me was planning to pull her closer. To forge a bond with her, I hadn't contemplated sharing with anyone in decades. And there I was, doing the very opposite. It stung, but it was the best choice for both of us.

six

PAIGE

"He's here," I whispered into my phone from the bath-room stall at Velocity.

"Who is?" Elle asked.

"Rhys."

"Who?"

I sighed. "The silver fox from the bar."

"No way. That's perfect. See, you two are meant to be. You should—"

I cut her off. "He's my boss."

She let out a little nervous laugh. "Oh no, Paige. *Oh shit.* The pictures! What are you going to do about the pictures?"

My heart raced. I'd forgotten about them. I hadn't told her what happened between him and me in the alleyway, but at least that only existed in our memories. The photos, however, were very real, and beyond inappropriate.

What was I going to do about them? They were no longer on a stranger's cell phone, which was bad enough, but rather on my boss's phone, which was much worse. Why had I done that? It was a foolish and risqué move, and of course, it had to come back to haunt me.

I leaned my head against the stall wall before I realized what I'd done and lifted it back up again, because, *gross.* "Guess I'm quitting. It's either that or I'll wait to get fired. Which is better?"

The door to the bathroom squeaked open, and I whispered to Elle that I had to go and hung up the phone.

I left the stall and recognized the redhead at the sink fixing her hair as another one of the new hires.

She turned to look at me. "Oh, it's *you.*"

I felt like I was in high school again, being assessed by one of the popular girls, and failing to make the grade.

Perfect, day one, and I already had someone who failed to understand that we were on the same team. This wasn't an internship. We all had positions of our own. There was no need for competition between us.

I didn't respond to her. What could I say to that? Best to ignore and move on.

She stopped, turned, and rested her palm on the counter. "Do you know Mr. Lockwood?"

A tingle ran through me. "What? No, why?"

"When you came into the room. *Late.* He knew your first name."

Oh, no. Think quick.

"How do you know he doesn't know us all by name? He owns a social media company. Do you think he hasn't looked us all up online?"

She tipped her head and pouted before nodding. She looked familiar, but I couldn't place her. "Okay, yeah, good point. Sorry," she said with a smile. "I'm Roxanne."

Her attitude took such a rapid one-eighty I might have

had whiplash.

"Paige, but I guess you knew that already."

"I did. Sorry, Paige. I didn't mean to have an attitude with you. I just hate injustice. I thought maybe you knew him, and you hadn't worked hard for the position like the rest of us. But that was unfair of me to assume. I feel ashamed of myself for jumping to conclusions like that. Us women have it hard enough in this world without turning on each other. Am I right?"

I nodded, feeling bad for not being honest with her from the start about how I'd met Rhys before. But I didn't know if I could trust her and that information didn't need to float around the office. Where did I know her from?

Roxanne? Roxy... Roxy Riot.

"You're Roxy Riot!"

She shushed me. "No, no, I'm not."

"Yes, you are." Her red hair, curvy body, and her face were unmistakable. She was an online body positivity influencer with a massive following and a track record for pissing off so many designers and corporations by protesting for inclusion.

She leaned in. "Okay, fine, I am, but can you keep it quiet, please?"

"Do they not know?"

She nodded. "Yes, they know. My online social presence is why they hired me, but they also asked me to keep it on the down low as much as possible for as long as possible."

"Why?"

"Because Fashion Sleek Boutique is one of their clients."

"I don't follow."

She sighed. "I *allegedly* ran a campaign that resulted in over 500 of their storefronts being vandalized last year."

"Allegedly?"

She turned back to the mirror and looked at me through the reflection, a mischievous smile on her lips. "That's what my lawyer told me to say."

"Wow, I'm surprised they hired you. Isn't that a conflict of interest?"

She shrugged. "Rhys Lockwood is notorious for hiring controversial people. Because we know how to sell ourselves and further a cause. Which is what we're here for, aren't we?"

She was right, and I felt inferior for it. What had I done? Sure, I'd studied hard at university, and graduated with honors, but all my accomplishments were on paper. I hadn't made a splash on social media. I'd probably end up shoved into a dusty basement somewhere in the bowels of the office building sorting mail. Especially with much more accomplished people like Roxy around. I couldn't compete with that, could I?

What was I even worrying about that for? I was going to be fired before the end of the week if I didn't get those pictures deleted. But how? Stealing his phone the first time was a breeze compared to what I'd have to do now. Not only would I have to get his phone, but I'd need the password to unlock it to get into his gallery.

Impossible. I might as well give up before I tried.

"Why the long face?"

I was startled by her voice, having forgotten that Roxy was there with me. "Oh, I'm fine, just first-day jitters."

She put her arm around my shoulders. "Well, you've got me now. Let's go rock this."

I laughed. It was something Elle would have said. Speaking of her, I'd have to call her back and brainstorm how we were going to fix this.

If it wasn't too late already.

seven

RHYS

"This area would be good to highlight." I pointed out a table in the corner with some artwork behind it to the Westwood representative. It looked like neon fireworks splashed over a black background. "It's intimate and fun. If we add a hip young couple, it should do the trick. I'll take a quick shot of it, a few other locations, and some interesting features to show our photographer." Westwood had other bars, including locations in Los Angeles, New York, and Boston that I'd need to visit with a team in the coming weeks.

I walked up to the bar and took a picture of the liquor bottles on display. It was a mandatory shot for any bar. I tried not to glance over at the now empty barstool that Paige occupied the other night.

I failed.

Dwelling on it would only make matters worse. I would have to appreciate what I couldn't have from a distance and hope my feelings for her would fade in time. I wasn't used to letting go after someone struck me as she had, but I had no other choice. Forget thick thighs save lives. She could have strangled me with hers and I would have died a lucky man.

Martin came through the door. "Hey bud, we've got a problem." He pulled me aside.

"What's going on?"

"The corporate head wants you in New York by the week's end. He went over the final contract and there are some terms he's being picky about. But once you go over them, he said he wants all the locations completed by the end of the month."

I flicked through the gallery of photos I'd taken. If I was heading out in a few days, I wanted to make sure I had everything I needed there first. "That's fine. We'll charter the jet. What's the problem, then?"

I kept flipping through the photos until I saw a closeup of the pretty face that had been haunting me.

Martin began answering my question. "Our team isn't..."

My attention waned.

What the fuck?

It was a video. My thumb hovered over the play button for a moment before I forced myself to ignore it and shoved the phone back into my pocket. It wasn't the time nor the place to be looking at whatever she had said in that video. I bit back a smile. Surprised she'd done that. She hadn't seemed like the type. And she hadn't mentioned it at all. Just left it for me like an Easter egg hunt. I wanted to see if there was more than one.

Even though I should have just deleted it, never to be thought of again.

Martin was still speaking, but I couldn't focus on his words.

I patted him on the back. "I've got somewhere I need to be. Fix it?"

"We need to assemble a new team."

"Make it happen."

"You got it, boss."

I made it all the way home through forty-five minutes of downtown Seattle traffic before pulling my phone from my pants pocket and setting it on my kitchen counter.

I paced.

Poured a Scotch.

Downed it.

Paced some more.

Whatever she had left behind was for *bar* me. Not for *boss* me.

I paused in a stare-down with my phone. But I *was* still the same person. The version of me she'd met the other night was me in my rawest form. The one who'd ended the evening with his hand up her skirt, with her breaking under my touch. I lifted the phone to my face and unlocked it.

No.

I set it back down.

I needed to blow off some steam. Fast.

Speed-walking down the hall to my room, I changed into my workout attire. A run on the treadmill would do the trick.

Then I'd delete it.

I couldn't watch it. Not now. It wasn't right.

But fuck, I wanted to.

It was just a still shot, but her smile captured me. It was already the most beautiful fucking video I'd ever seen, and I hadn't pressed play yet. I hopped on the treadmill that looked out over the city below from my modern penthouse suite. Mashed a few buttons, and the belt engaged. I ran a few steps.

Faster.

I upped the speed. Ran a few paces more.

Faster, still.

I couldn't focus on the city below like usual. It held no allure. Not with every brain cell focused on watching that video.

Faster.

Fuck it.

I hopped off the belt, leaving it speeding along without me, and crossed the room to the kitchen counter. Unlocked my phone, opened the gallery, and pressed play.

"Hey Rhys, I know you won't see this right away, and who knows, you might be married with children by this point. But I wanted to say that I enjoyed meeting you, and if you are still single, call me." She rattled off her phone number, her voice wavering a bit and stumbling over the last two digits. *"I also want you to know I never do stuff like this. So, yeah... call me? Oh, and I hope you enjoy the pictures."* She seemed unsure of herself through most of the video but finished it off by blowing me a quick kiss.

What pictures was she referring to? Were there more?

There had to be.

I slid my thumb to the right, over the glass screen.

She stood her round ass in the frame, with her dress hiked up just enough to let the bottom of each luscious cheek peek out from beneath the hem. I threw my phone on the counter.

My cock twitched.

She'd said pictures. Which meant there were others.

I. Wanted. More.

It was wrong of me, and I had no right to want more, but I couldn't help it.

I picked up the phone again and slid my finger over her ass, watching it disappear as a shot of her leaning toward the camera with her dress pulled down, and her arm wrapped across her chest. There was a glimpse of her pink areola between her fingertips.

As turned on as I was, this was a fucking reckless move on her part. She took the photos at the bar. Before our kiss. Or our date. Yet there she was in a compromising shot, her face in plain view. What the fuck was she thinking?

In the wrong hands, these were dangerous photos. I'd seen it often enough on social media. It's a sick world out there. As much as a woman should have been able to do as she pleased with her body without repercussions, we hadn't quite reached that nirvana state in society.

No, I was the sick one. After all, I was the one ogling pictures of my employee.

But I couldn't stop myself. She'd left them for me, after all. And there was no way in hell I'd ever let anyone catch even the tiniest glimpse of her perfect body.

I moved on to the next one. She was looking over her shoulder with every delicious curve in full view.

I reached down and adjusted my cock before moving on to the next. I burst out laughing. The next picture was just a selfie of her face, her tongue sticking out at me. I flipped again. That was it. The last, or the first one, as the case was.

I flipped back and forth through them more times than I could count, watching her go from cute to sexy and back again. My interest grew to the point where if I'd been any harder, I might have punched a hole through my workout shorts with my dick.

I settled on the photo of her ass peeking out from beneath the hem of her dress and reached my hand into the waistband of my shorts, wrapping it around my shaft. As I traced the curve of her cheeks with my eyes, I gave it a few pumps. I imagined placing my hand between her shoulder blades and pushing her down and forward until her pussy stared back at me between those thick, meaty thighs of hers.

I wondered what it would look like in reality. Would she be wet for me? How would she feel wrapped around me as I plunged deep into her? I squeezed tighter, pumping faster at the thought of her young cunt enveloping my thick cock. I wished I could grab onto her hips and take her hard and fast until she screamed my name and came undone with me deep inside her. And I would just hold her to me for a while after, my cock still buried in her, relishing in how perfect it was to leave my mark on her body.

Fuck.

I ripped my hand from my shorts and away from my throbbing cock, robbing it of release. My fingers were sticky from pre-cum.

I'd gone way too far.

Way, way too far.

I set down my phone and headed for the bathroom to shower.

If I'd wanted her before, and I had, I'd just made it a lot fucking worse. Nothing like that could ever happen again. Especially not in the flesh.

I turned the shower on and cranked the tap until the water ran hot enough to scorch my skin. Once done, I went straight back to my phone, without bothering to towel off first, and deleted everything she'd left on it.

What happened earlier could never happen again, and as much as I might have liked to keep them, it was my work phone. My only phone, but still my work phone. It wasn't the place for photos like that, especially incriminating ones. I hoped between the shower and deleting them I'd washed away every trace of what I wanted to do with her—*to her*.

Only time would tell.

eight

PAIGE

Thud.

A stack of files appeared on my desk from out of Roxy's hands next to the stack from yesterday, which I was only just finishing up. "Mr. Lockwood sent these for you."

I threw my head back. When was he going to ease up on me? It was only Wednesday, and he'd been piling extra work on me every day. What was he trying to prove? Was he trying to get me to quit?

I didn't want to lose my position with Velocity, but it was becoming clear he wasn't feeling the same. And, to make matters worse, I hadn't even been close enough to him to do something about the photos. He was keeping his distance, but still making his presence known.

I didn't want to quit, but if he kept it up, I'd have no choice.

It was *torture*. I was getting twice the work of the other new hires.

"Thanks," I said.

She gave me a sympathetic smile and slid what remained of yesterday's files off of my desk. "I'll take care of these for you."

"You don't have to do that."

"We're in this together, remember?"

"Thank you," I mouthed to her.

Roxy had been nothing short of amazing since our encounter in the bathroom. She had a bit of a quick-to-rise temper that I'd seen her take out on a jammed copier on the second day. But she always brought me something back when she went on break since I often refused to leave my desk. I had no choice if I was going to make it through the work I was being given.

She started walking away. "Oh, I almost forgot. He said to start with the third file."

What a bizarre request. Why not put the files in order of urgency?

I removed the first two files from the stack and flipped open the third file. There was a sticky note stuck to a blank sheet.

See me in my office.

My heart thumped in my chest. This was it. I was going to lose my job over a freak incident. Why did it have to be my boss in the bar that night? Why had I let a stranger put his hand up my dress in an alley? The photos were the least of my worries now, but maybe this was my chance to get rid of them. Elle had suggested I dress more provocatively and see if I caught his attention enough to get close to him.

If the note was any sign, my best friend was also an evil genius.

The nauseous feeling I'd been living with all week grew

stronger as I stood. Roxy looked up from her desk over at me. I tried to look calm, like my heart wasn't beating so hard it was moments away from bursting out of my chest.

The one time, *the one freaking time* I took a risk. It backfired. I couldn't help but worry. It was about to get much worse. He was going to fire me. I knew it. How was I going to afford to stay in Seattle while I looked for another job? My dad already wanted me to 'stop this foolishness' and go to work for him, but that wasn't what I wanted. I wanted to make something of myself—by myself. I didn't want to use his celebrity or reputation. This was why I concealed my last name while applying for jobs. It wasn't a lie. I'd just omitted half of my hyphenated surname. I'd chosen to go by Wilkins instead of Stanley when I started university. My father's last name was too recognizable with his celebrity.

I glanced at the alcove of elevators.

Maybe I wouldn't go to his office. I could put it off. Pretend I wasn't at my desk when Roxy came by. But I didn't want to risk getting her in trouble.

Then again, if I put it off long enough, maybe this would all blow over...

I knew I was insane for even thinking about it, though.

The time we spent in the alley was unforgettable for me. Didn't he feel the same? Or had I misread his intentions?

There was only one way to find out.

I crumpled the note and tossed it in the recycling bin under my desk and made my way over to his office. The door was closed, and his assistant's desk was vacant. Maybe she took an early lunch? With any luck, he'd joined her. I knocked on his door.

"Come in," he called out from within.

Turning the knob, I felt like I was on my way to my execution. I opened the door and took a tentative step into the room. He looked up from his desk. His gaze was serious. Unreadable. Those ice-blue eyes held none of the magic they once had.

"Close the door behind you—" He dropped his voice. "—and lock it."

I did as he asked and turned around, clasping my hands behind my back.

"Come over here."

The clack of the red heels Elle had convinced me to wear echoed in the oversized office as I approached him. I stopped behind the chair, as though it might shield me from what was about to happen.

My heart was racing. He wore a stern expression on his face. Any playfulness that he'd shown me the other night was gone. I couldn't believe he was the same guy who had charmed me the first time we met. He'd pulled feelings from me I thought I'd never have about anyone. Where was that man? The desire to dissipate into thin air overcame me.

The sad part was. I still wanted him. It was tough to let go of the man he had shown me that night. I knew he was in there, but could I get to him again? Or was he off-limits to me?

"You wanted to see me?" I asked, breaking the silence between us.

"I did, yes." He stood from his chair and paced the floor. "You're driving me crazy, Paige."

"What do you mean?"

He ran his hand over his face. "What happened to the schoolteacher garb?"

I looked down at my outfit. "Am I violating the dress code?"

He stepped toward me.

"Well, no, but…" He paced some more instead of finishing his thought and I stepped back toward the door to keep my distance and hopefully escape unscathed.

He knew as well as I did that he had no good reason for calling me into his office.

"Is that all you wanted, Mr. Lockwood?"

He shook his head, stalking closer to me as I backed away.

"Because I have a lot of work to do, and I should get back to it now. *Someone* keeps giving me extra files." I held back a smile. I could see the want in his eyes. The internal battle between what was appropriate and what he wanted warred within him, and he wasn't hiding it well.

I reached out for the doorknob, and he cut me off, closing the gap between us. He backed me up against the wall, pinned my one arm overhead, and placed his other palm flat against the wall, caging me in. My heart leaped.

He shook his head. "I gave you extra work because you're good at what you do, Paige."

That was why? I'd completely misread his intentions. And it might have made me feel proud to know he felt that way, but my professional performance was the furthest thing from my mind at that moment.

He glanced at my lips. "We can't do this, you know."

His face was so close to mine that it wouldn't have taken much to kiss away his protests. "I know, Mr. Lockwood." My voice was breathy and quiet.

Being up against the wall made me think back to being in the alley with him. A heatwave overcame me as I remembered his hand between my thighs as his fingers penetrated me. The overwhelming pleasure I felt when he made me come. His face was so close I could feel his breath on my skin, and it was electrifying. I'd never felt that way about any man before. The pull between us was magnetic, the space between us unwelcome.

"You might need a custom dress code." He wet his bottom lip with his tongue. "If we're going to make this work without incident. I need you to cover up more."

"Do you think that will help, Sir?"

His eyes fell to my cleavage. "No."

With the outline visible in his dress pants, I could tell that he was hard. I moved my body forward enough to brush up against his erection. "I'll do anything you need—to help."

What had come over me?

Was I trying to seduce my boss?

"Anything, baby girl?"

I nodded. "Anything."

"Have you ever sucked a cock before?"

I bit my lip. It felt like a trick question, but I had to answer him honestly. "I have, sort of."

"Would you like to again?"

"As long as it's yours, yes."

He let out a huff of a laugh. "Do you think I'd ask you to suck anyone else's cock, beautiful?"

"Well, no, It's just—"

"On your knees."

A gush of wetness hit my panties at his forceful words, but I couldn't force my body to obey. He'd done a complete shift since I'd entered his office. From cold to hot. His once icy eyes were molten, and all that heat flowed my way. But were we about to make a huge mistake?

"Paige, are you listening to me? Or do I have to bend you over my desk and make you listen?"

My breath hitched, and I mustered a nod. "I'm listening to you, Mr. Lockwood. I'm listening to every word."

"Call me Rhys."

"Pardon me, Mr. Lockwood, but I don't think that's appropriate. We should keep things professional. Don't you think?"

"Fuck, I'm trying. I am. But then you showed up. Wearing those heels and that dress. I'm losing it having you so close, yet so out of reach. I'm losing the will to stay away from you, and it was already hanging on by a thread."

My will to resist him was gone in an instant, hearing that he'd been feeling the same way about me as I had him.

"Then lose it. I want you to."

"I don't know how things can work between us. You deserve to be shown off. But I can't give that to you, Paige. In a perfect world, I wouldn't have to be saying any of this. Or tucking notes into file folders to speak with you. I wouldn't be here wishing I could lean you back on my desk and steal a taste of you."

My thoughts scrambled and unscrambled. He wanted me as much as I did him. We needed to make this easy on ourselves. Why try to resist when it was clear we would only fail? "It can be a perfect world of another definition, Rhys..."

He shook his head.

"No, don't give up. We just have to keep it to ourselves. No one else needs to know. I don't care about being paraded around. All I care about is spending more time with you."

"You say that now. Until you're crying about the injustice of it all. Until you're crying because we can never be, and we dragged it on for far too long. I can't take any more from you, Paige. I've already taken too much. Not when I know there's a chance that I won't be able to give you everything I want in return. But, fuck, I want to."

"I'll quit then. Right here. Right now."

"And then what?"

"I'll get a dead-end job until something better comes along."

He shook his head. "There's nothing better for you than the opportunity you have here at Velocity."

That wasn't true. "I'll go work for my father. He wants me to anyhow, he's—"

"Stop." He slapped his hand on the wall and I jumped. "This isn't a negotiation. You're not throwing away your future for me. Do you understand me?"

"What about what I want?"

"What you want and what you need are two different things. I told you the night we met you didn't know what you needed out of life yet. This is proof of that."

Ouch.

"I don't appreciate being treated like a child, Rhys. You can't decide for me, especially when they're not even the decisions you want to be making."

He groaned. "Fuck, I'm going to kiss you now, Paige, so if you have a problem with that, now would be the time to—"

I didn't give him the chance to finish his sentence and instead threw my arms around his neck, kissing him. He dropped his arm, wrapping it around my waist, and pulled my body flush to his. His kisses traveled from my lips to my neck. "I can't stand—" He continued kissing. "—being around you and not touching you."

We may have been making a huge mistake, but there was nothing we could do to stop it. I dropped to my knees. I was about to show him just how much I appreciated him bending his will for me.

Three quick raps on the door caused Rhys to jump back.

"Mr. Lockwood? Mr. Henrick is here to see you." His assistant's voice said through the door.

He helped me to my feet. "Fuck. You've got to hide. I meant to get you out of here before she got back," he said, his voice hushed. He darted to the closet, opening it. "Get in here."

"I—I can't."

He came back to me, ushering me toward the closet. "Baby, I'll make it quick, I promise."

"I'm not good with—"

He planted a firm kiss on my lips. "I'll get you out of here unnoticed soon." He gave me one last gentle push and closed the door, plunging me into darkness.

I wanted to tell him I wasn't good in confined spaces, but he didn't give me the chance.

My heart hammered in my ears as I sank to the floor, my breathing almost deafening in the small space.

I wanted out more than anything.

But I'd also told him I could do this—that we could be a secret. Bursting out of the closet would bring a premature end to that promise.

I pressed my hands to the walls and shut my eyes, trying to prevent the closet from enveloping me even more.

He said he wouldn't be long.

I had to hang on—*for us.*

nine

RHYS

I wrapped up the meeting as fast as I could. The question was, how was I going to get Paige out of the closet unnoticed? I called Naomi into my office.

She rounded the corner. "Yes, Mr. Lockwood?"

"I realized we're overdue for a fire drill."

"Oh, you're right, we are. Shall I plan for one later this week?"

"No, let's do it now."

"Now? Like right now?"

"Yes. Is that a problem?"

"No. Of course not, Mr. Lockwood. It's just we've never done one without notice before."

"I'll be out of the office later this week. So, I want to do it now. Get on with it."

I waved my hand, signaling for her to leave my office.

"I'll do the last sweep. You're in charge of the count downstairs."

"Yes, Sir."

Naomi left my office, and I shut the door, locking it behind her.

I went to the closet to open the door. The fire alarm rang out overhead just as the door flew open and Paige came out. She had streaks of mascara running down her face, and she was as pale as a ghost. Was she startled by the deafening noise? She glanced at the office door and tried to bypass me.

I took her by the shoulders. "Wait until the others clear out. Then you can go."

She stopped, but she wouldn't look up at me. Her body trembled in my hands.

"Are you okay?" I slid my arms around her, hugging her.

She didn't respond. Could she not hear me? Or did she just not want to respond?

It was clear something was off with her.

Her body was rigid against mine. She didn't push away, but I felt she wanted to. Placing my hand over her ear, I pressed her other ear to my chest to protect them from the sharp tone of the fire alarm. After a minute passed, I could feel her body give in to my hold. She closed her eyes and returned my hug.

She tipped her head back, looking up at me with those doe eyes of hers, and I wiped her mascara away with my thumb. Something had upset her, but it wasn't the time nor the place to get into it. People would expect us downstairs, and the shrill alarm made conversing for any length of time impossible.

I crossed the room and peeked out the door. There wasn't anyone in sight. "Okay, you need to go now."

"Okay." I could see her mouth the word, but her voice was so quiet I couldn't hear her. She hurried out the door.

Something had her spooked, but the question was what?

Had she changed her mind about us? Did her first taste of being a hidden woman not sit well with her? I knew it was too good to be true that we could give this a shot. I needed to prevent her from getting hurt any further, even if it meant doing the last thing I wanted to do.

Downstairs, at the muster point, I did my best not to look over at her. The last thing we needed was for people to figure us out when things were over before they'd begun.

Martin came up to me. "You gotta let a guy know about these things. I was in the middle of an important call, Rhys."

I shrugged. "Sorry about that."

Even though I'd have done it all over again if I had to.

I saw the redhead, Roxy, talking to Paige in a hushed tone. She glanced over her shoulder at me and rolled her eyes before looking away.

What was her sudden attitude about? I'd have to monitor her. She had a reputation for causing trouble. I'd be a fool to think that having her on my payroll afforded me any kind of immunity.

Martin moved to stand beside me. I cleared my throat and turned to find Naomi. She was across the way from me. "Has the count been done?" I called out to her.

"Yup, we're all accounted for."

"Okay, great job everyone. Back to work."

I watched Paige out of the corner of my eye. This whole thing was too much. I couldn't be conducting a fire drill every time they almost caught us. And I couldn't deal with her looking as upset as she did when she came out of my closet. She didn't deserve that.

It was clear what I had to do, even if I didn't want to.

I had to let her go.

ten

PAIGE

The blonde woman I recognized as Naomi, Rhys's assistant, poked her head into my cubicle. "Can I borrow you for a few minutes?"

"Of course." I swiveled out of my chair to follow her.

Rhys was out of the office again. I'd texted him after I got off work the day of the fire drill—okay—the day she'd almost caught us together in his office.

I apologized for how I'd reacted and told him I'd explain everything. But when he texted me back, he said he was sorry, but we couldn't do this. I was getting iced out again. Was he sending his assistant to deliver the bad news that he was firing me? Maybe he knew he needed me out of the office, but he couldn't bear to do it himself.

What if he'd seen the pictures?

Then again, did they even matter anymore? We'd been close to doing a lot worse in his office. But knowing they existed gave me an icky feeling in my gut that I couldn't seem to shake, no matter how hard I tried.

We reached Naomi's desk.

"Okay, so this is pretty unconventional, and you can say no if you want to, but I remembered when I was screening resumes. You had photography listed as one of your hobbies. Is that right?"

"Yes, that's right." It was almost ten in the morning, and he still wasn't in the office. I wondered if this was normal or maybe the other day was such an embarrassment to him, that he'd skipped work. I knew I'd thought about it the night before.

"So, Paige, we're in a bit of a pickle."

"Oh?"

Pickle? Did people still say that? She couldn't have been that much older than I was.

"Our photographer and her team moved on. We're under some budget constraints this quarter because of a new acquisition. So, we aren't outsourcing at the moment. This leaves us without a photographer at present. What kind of photography do you do?"

She couldn't be serious, could she? Was she about to ask me to step in for a professional photographer? Sure, I'd dreamed about being a photographer long before I went to school for marketing, but it seemed like such a long shot to make a career out of it.

"A few weddings. Some nature. Not any landscape," I answered.

I enjoyed taking portraits. People, animals, and insects. It didn't matter as long as it was alive and dynamic.

"We don't have any use for landscape. Just some model shots and closeups of interesting things."

"I could handle that."

"Are you free this weekend? We will comp your meals and hotel, of course, and even though you aren't eligible for it yet, we're committing to paying you overtime for all hours spent working."

"Hotel?"

Naomi laughed. "I guess I should have mentioned that we'll need you to fly to New York. You'd leave tom…"

Her words faded away, though her lips kept moving. Fly? I'd flown lots before, but I never got used to it. My throat was already getting tight at the thought of spending however many hours trapped thirty-thousand feet in the air.

Naomi tipped her head. "We have a client that—are you okay?"

Was it that obvious I was freaking out? This was a perfect opportunity for me to impress, and considering my office dungeon worries, how could I turn it down?

I forced a smile. "Great. I'm great. Can't wait."

"Oh—oh! You'll do it, then? Perfect. A car will pick you up and transport you to the tarmac in the morning."

"I can get myself to the airport."

She laughed. "You're not flying commercial. We don't have that kind of time to waste."

"I see. Is anyone else going with me?"

"No, well, besides Mr. Lockwood and myself, of course."

I froze. Did he know I was going?

How would he feel about it?

"Maybe, uh, maybe you should get someone else to do it."

She furrowed her brow. "Is it because the boss is going? I know he seems intimidating, but Rhys is great. He always does his best to make people feel welcome."

Maybe that was true for most people. But after the response to my text, I was certain it wouldn't be true for me. But maybe this is what I needed? A weekend's worth of chances to get a hold of his phone and delete the embarrassing photos before he saw them. At least then I could get rid of the sick feeling in the pit of my stomach once and for all. Assuming that was the only thing about the arrangement that I felt sick over.

"Yeah, okay. Sorry, I'm just new. It's intimidating."

"Nothing to be intimidated about. You'll do great. I'm sure of it." She licked a fingertip and flipped through some paperwork before pausing and looking up at me. "Unless you lied on your resume."

I laughed. "No, I didn't." The photography was just about the only part of the pending trip that I wasn't worried about.

Spending the weekend working side-by-side with a distant Rhys was going to be a lot to handle.

Then again, maybe I was misreading the entire situation. Had he created this opportunity for us?

He came around the corner, coffee in hand, his cold gaze locked on mine for only a moment, before he looked away and slipped into his office. A shiver ran down my spine.

This was going to be tougher than I thought.

eleven

RHYS

"What do you mean, you can't make it? Naomi, I..."

She started rattling on about how her son had her up all night with some stomach bug. How her babysitter was refusing to take him and how she was worried she might have caught it. I felt like a dick for even making her explain herself like that.

As the son of a single mother growing up, I knew she was a parent first. I always tried my best to understand that for any of the parents that worked for me.

"That's fine. Tell Josh I hope he feels better soon." She thanked me and yelled something about a bucket before the line disconnected.

Just perfect.

One of our biggest contracts of the year was riding on this and there I was, showing up with an inexperienced skeleton staff. I didn't even get the chance to ask her who was coming. I thought about calling her back, but she had her hands full enough without me adding my worries about the weekend ahead to it. Knowing her, she already felt bad enough for falling through on her commitment. She was the best assistant I'd ever had.

I heard the crew welcoming other passengers aboard. I sat up in my chair.

That's when I saw Paige come around the corner.

I sucked in a sharp breath. She looked as stunning as ever. Her long dark hair and lashes. Those brown eyes had stamped my soul the moment we met. I knew I'd never shake it even if I lived a thousand years.

But I had to.

"Hi, Mr. Lockwood," she said as she slid into the seat across from mine. She was wearing another dress. Her bare legs turned my thoughts dirty in an instant. My eyes trailed up her body to the curve of her subtle cleavage. I couldn't help but wonder what would have happened if I had her on her knees again with no one to interrupt us.

I turned my head to look out the window. Images of her photographs flashed through my mind. The guilt of what I'd done returned. What we'd almost done in my office. How was I going to endure this? She was too fucking sexy for her own good. With hips and an ass just begging to bear my children.

Fuck.

Stop, Rhys, just stop it.

"Hi," I said, knowing I should turn my gaze from her, but failing to.

"I—I thought Naomi would be here already."

"She's not coming. We're just waiting on the others now."

"There are others? She said it'd just be the three of us."

My veins turned to fire and ice at the same time as a thrill tainted with fear coursed through me.

Was I hearing her correctly? A weekend alone with Paige?

This was bad.

Bad. Fucking. News.

But also, the best news I'd received since she'd crashed into me in the boardroom.

Paige and I sat in silence while the crew prepped for take-off. There was so much I'd planned to say to her before I knew she was my employee. So many things I wanted to do with her the next time I got her alone.

A far less wise man might have called our situation fate. Or thought that the universe was forcing us together. While I may not have been the wisest man, I was smart enough to know that fate could also be cruel.

Was it a test?

I shook my head, and she looked over at me. We locked eyes as the plane aligned itself with the runway to make its ascent into the sky.

My eyes dropped to her hands. Her knuckles were white from gripping the armrests of her chair.

"Do I make you that nervous?"

She followed my gaze to her hands and let go, folding them in her lap instead.

"No. I'm a nervous flyer."

"Did you bring anything for it? Anti-nausea medication?"

She was startled as the plane picked up the pace for take-off. "It's not what you'd expect. It's just when the doors close and I think about how trapped we are until the plane lands I get—"

"Anxious?"

"Yes, but it's more of a suffocating feeling."

"It sounds like claustrophobia to me. My mother had that. We had a kitchen pantry that I always had to stock and retrieve things from because the door swung closed on its own, and she couldn't stand being in there."

Paige gave me a weak smile. Perhaps telling her about more confined spaces while in a confined space wasn't the brightest move. That's when it hit me. I'd shoved her into a fucking closet the other day. Her tears, her pale freaked out expression, it all made sense now. She wasn't regretting us, she was claustrophobic, and I'd stuffed her in a confined space.

I felt like a huge ass for how I responded to her text. I should have asked her what she was thinking instead of assuming I knew what she wanted. It was more or less what she'd warned me not to do and I'd gone and done it again.

As the plane took off and her body tensed, her breathing became shallow and rapid. I glanced up at the illuminated seatbelt sign and groaned. How many rules was I willing to break for this woman?

All of them.

I unbuckled, and she sucked in a breath.

"Rhys! What are you doing?"

I moved around the table and sat next to her, buckling back up. I pried her hands apart and wrapped one in my palms.

"Are you afraid of heights?"

"Not really. Why?"

"Perfect. Just listen to me and do as I tell you, okay?"

Her lips were tight, but she nodded.

"Look out the window. Get your face nice and close. I

want you to focus only on what you see outside. Can you do that?"

"Yeah, but I—"

"Tell me what you see, Paige."

"Umm, clouds?"

"Good. What else?"

"The sun?"

"What else?"

"That's it. There's nothing else."

"There's one thing you're missing. One very important thing. Look closer, baby girl."

The term of endearment caused her head to spin in my direction, her wide eyes full and bright in the sunlight that shone into the cabin.

"Eyes on the window. What else is out there?"

She shook her head and shrugged, searching through the window for the answer. "Uh, there's nothing but open sky. That's it..."

She gasped, and that's when I knew she'd seen it. I'd been coaching her to shift her perspective. To see that the world was still big. Still there for her. She may have been trapped in a sense, but there was a wider world waiting for her after our short ride.

I leaned forward, pressing my chest to her back, wrapping my arms around her to hold her as we sat staring out the window together. Once her breathing slowed, she relaxed into me with a soft sigh.

"I'm okay now. Thank you for that."

She twisted in my arms, her face only inches from mine. Those lips. I was desperate to feel them again, and they begged to be kissed. Lips I had no business tasting again. I ran my thumb over her cheek, my eyes locked on hers as I slipped my fingers into her hair, cupping the back of her neck.

There was nothing I wouldn't do to make her more comfortable. To make sure that I protected her from every worry or fear that she had. My lips descended on hers, sealing my silent oath with a kiss.

twelve

PAIGE

We arrived in time for lunch. Rhys and I checked into our rooms and parted ways long enough to get settled and meet back down in the foyer of the New York location of the Stanley Hotel.

He changed into jeans and pushed the sleeves of his Henley shirt up, revealing his muscular forearms. The casual look was much closer to the man I'd met at the bar that night than my suited-up boss. We didn't have any meetings scheduled until the morning. Though I wasn't sure why. It felt odd to be paid overtime for a non-working day, but I wasn't about to complain.

"We'll have to go elsewhere to eat. The hotel restaurant's booked solid with reservations."

He did not know who I was, or rather, who my father was. Or that we were staying at one of my dad's hotels. It amused me because I'd never been a paying guest in one before. Not that I was paying for it, but I assumed they had, of course. It was also bizarre for me to be staying in anything less than an executive suite. But I was just in a standard room, and it felt like a dose of the normal I'd been hoping for when I took the job with Velocity instead of going to work for my father.

I knew the restaurant would make space for us. The private dining room that my father insisted on having in all his restaurants would be available to us. All I had to do was show my face and someone would recognize me. But I didn't want to spoil the occasion.

"That's okay. I'm sure we can find something. I hear the food trucks are amazing in New York."

He wrapped his arm around my waist. "Now you're speaking my language." We headed for the door.

There was something so grounded about him, and I could tell he hadn't grown up with much money. He was a self-made man, I was sure of it, and it was an attractive quality. He didn't come from the same old money that my family ran on that had catapulted my father to fame. No, Rhys didn't reek of privilege like the boys I'd gone to school with, and it was sexy to know that everything he had he'd worked for. It's what I wanted for myself. It might have been a work weekend, but I was more interested to see what it had in store for the two of us.

The front door to the hotel swung open as a familiar couple burst through it, bickering away, when the man just stopped, grabbed her, and pulled her in for a passionate kiss. My heart sank, and I pulled away from Rhys's hold before they had the chance to notice us. My sister turned, smoothing out her dress as she recovered from the public manhandling her French fiancé had given her. When Bianca saw me, she squealed and rushed forward to hug me.

"Paige, what are you doing here?"

"Work stuff." I glanced over at Rhys, his head tipped to

the side as he eyed me during the exchange. I sighed. So much for my hidden identity.

"Bee, this is my boss Rhys Lockwood, Rhys this is my sister Bianca and her fiancé Andre Auclair." They all shook hands and exchanged pleasantries.

Bianca brushed her blonde curls over her shoulder. "Were you headed out? We were just about to have lunch."

Rhys smiled. "We were. The hotel restaurant is full, so we were just going to find somewhere else to eat."

Bianca crinkled her nose. "Why wouldn't you just use Dad's table?" She waved her hand. "Doesn't matter. There is plenty of room for all of us. Come along." She hooked her arm in Andre's and motioned for us to follow them.

Rhys held me back and leaned over, dropping his voice. "Paige, who's your daddy?"

I was tempted to be cheeky and tell Rhys that he was. He'd called himself that in the alleyway, after all. But I decided against it.

"Horace Stanley."

He furrowed his brow at me. "I thought your last name was Wilkins?"

"It is, well, one of them is. My full last name is Wilkins-Stanley." I chewed at my bottom lip, waiting for his reply. I knew they were likely to look up who I was when I started looking for a job. Omitting my father's last name was the best chance I had at getting hired based on my merit, and not just because of who he was.

He pulled me close to him and let out a low growl. "I don't like it when I don't know who I'm involved with, Paige." His face was so close to mine.

"I'm sorry. But you didn't seem to mind not knowing much about me that night in the alley—or even a few minutes ago."

"Hmm, point taken." He smiled. "It's okay, we have all weekend to get to know each other better. Would you like that, baby girl?"

My heart hammered in my chest. Like it? I couldn't think of anything better. Even though everything might end when we returned to Seattle—to the office—I didn't care. I wanted every stolen moment I could get.

"I'd love it."

thirteen

RHYS

I couldn't take my eyes off Paige throughout lunch. My hunger was insatiable in ways that food, no matter how delicious, couldn't even touch. There was something so right about being next to her.

We fit.

I was so fucking sprung this woman, I almost didn't know what to do with myself. I was hyper-aware of her every movement, every brush of our body parts above and below the table. It made me wish we were alone so I could grab her and kiss her as silly as she made me feel.

Her sister and her fiancé bickered over the menu. Andre started rattling off something in French while Bianca giggled like that was what she hoped would happen when she got him all riled up. He shook his head and reached out for her hand, kissing it with a smile.

They didn't seem to mind showing affection in public, but Paige and I weren't at that point yet. We might make it there someday. The limited time we had over the two-day weekend seemed like the prime opportunity to explore that, but meeting her family wasn't a part of the plan. I couldn't wait to get her alone again.

I still didn't know what all of this would mean come Monday morning. When we would be back in the office. But if there was even a slight chance we could end up together, I'd do everything I could to make that happen for us.

Bianca folded her hands on the table, her expression serious. "What's going on between you two?"

Paige gasped, "Bee, you can't just ask something like that. He's my boss."

"And you're my little sister. I know something is going on. He can't take his eyes off of you." Bianca glanced over at me, and I just shrugged. It was up to Paige to decide how much she wanted to say to her sister.

Paige side-eyed me. "I'll let you know when I know."

That wasn't the answer I was hoping she'd give. But what could I expect? We hadn't defined our relationship. If we could even call it that.

Bianca quirked a brow, looking every bit as dissatisfied by Paige's answer as I felt. The two girls couldn't have been more opposite in looks. Bianca was blonde-haired with blue eyes and Paige had stunning, honey brown eyes and chestnut hair. The only thing they had in common was that they were both very curvaceous. But even their shapes differed. Paige was more petite up top with wider hips and an ass that made me want to take a bite out of it every time she turned around.

Bianca focused her attention on me. "And you? What are your intentions with my sister?"

To keep her forever.

I wrapped my arm around Paige's shoulder. Bianca had exposed us, so there was no point in trying to keep my hands to myself any longer. "I intend to help her figure it out."

Paige looked over at me with a hint of a smile on her luscious lips. Bianca was correct, I'd been staring, and I didn't care who noticed. We finished up our food, and I excused myself, telling Paige I'd see her later. They refused to let me pay the bill on the way out. Anyone who sat at the table didn't pay, as ordered by Horace Stanley, Paige and Bianca's father. I left a generous tip instead.

"Wait," Paige said, dashing out into the hotel lobby behind me. "I'm sorry if my sister upset you."

Is that what she thought?

"She didn't. Besides, she's your sister and is dating your dad's best friend. I'm sure she will use discretion and not tell anyone what she knows."

Paige nodded. "What are we even doing, Rhys? Once this weekend is over, I mean."

"I can't answer that. The company has a strict no-dating policy. How would it look if I was the one to break it? It's my policy after all. As much as I care for you, I'm not prepared to introduce chaos back into Velocity. Whatever we've done and decide to do going forward, will need to be between us only. I understand if that's not something that interests you."

"I don't care who knows. Or in this case, doesn't know."

"Are you sure? It's harder being someone's secret than you might think."

"I'm sure."

I stepped toward her, wrapping my arms around her waist. Her thick, curvy body felt right close to mine. I'd been mapping it since the moment we'd met, and I was more than ready to set sail and explore every inch of her. "Do you want to head upstairs for a bit? Or would you rather tour the city?"

She laughed. "I've been to New York more times than I can count. Let's go upstairs."

"Meet me in my room in thirty minutes. Wear something comfortable."

fourteen

PAIGE

I knocked on the door of Rhys's hotel room. I may have been in a standard room, but he wasn't. The floor number told me he was in one of our business executive suites. My stomach was in my throat. I looked down at the leggings and oversized t-shirt I'd worn. He said to wear something more comfortable. Was that code for something sexy? I hadn't come prepared for anything except work and casual nights in my room.

He opened the door and scanned my body. His lips twitched into a smile. All he wore were gray lounge pants. His bare chest was smooth except for a small patch of graying chest hair. The moment the door clicked closed behind me, Rhys's lips were on mine. He spun me, backing me toward the living area of the suite he was in. A suite designed by the very sister that was questioning us downstairs. She'd done what my father had asked. She worked for him. I chose Velocity. I chose Rhys, and it was hard to feel any regret about that with his arms around me and his tongue between my lips.

He groaned into my mouth as we fell back onto the sofa, his groin pressing into me. The hard outline of his cock was noticeable between my legs. He reared back. "We need to talk about your virginity."

I sat up, scanning the room. There were no less than a dozen candles along the mantle. An enormous bouquet of roses was on the table next to a bottle of champagne on ice. Okay, yeah, he had meant for me to wear something sexy. I tugged at my shirt, feeling more than a little self-conscious about missing the message. "What about it?"

He sat forward, popped the cork on the champagne, and poured two glasses before setting the bottle back on ice.

"Haven't you been—saving it?"

I rolled my eyes. What was it with men assuming that just because I was over twenty and a virgin I was saving myself? My status as a virgin had nothing to do with purity or chastity. "No, nothing like that. I've just never felt like anyone was the right one until..." How would he respond to me telling him he was the one? The one that changed it all. I looked down at the floor.

He took my chin between his finger and thumb. "Look at me. I don't want to hurt you. I'm feeling how you're feeling, Paige, but..."

"Stop."

"Stop, what?"

"Trying to protect me from this. From us. I realize things may not work out between us and I'm willing to accept that risk with you—to be with you."

He frowned. "You say that now. If things can't work out between us, I don't want you to feel used. I couldn't live with myself knowing I'd hurt you like that. That I'd taken more from you than I should have." He took my hands in his and stared into my eyes. "I've waited my whole life for a woman like you. I'll just spend the night with you, holding you. We can watch a movie. We don't have to do this. Not yet. Not until the time is right. I'll wait as long as it takes for you. For us."

"Do you think that would hurt me any less? I don't want to wait for a day that may never come because I don't want to lose you. We are in this together, Rhys, whether you like it or not. From the moment we met, we were already in too deep to walk away from this without it hurting. You know that as well as I do."

He nodded, almost imperceptibly as he chewed on my words. "So, what now?"

I hesitated for a moment before I moved to straddle him and wrapped my arms around his neck. "We make the most of the time we've been given."

The pure hunger in his eyes as he slid his hands around my hips, grabbed my ass, and pulled me to him sent a jolt of excitement through me. I squirmed on his lap as I felt his length grow hard beneath me, feeling more than ready to give myself to him.

All of our indecision led back to the same place every time. We were incapable of accepting a scenario where I wasn't his and he wasn't mine. As much as we may have tried to protest, it couldn't have been any other way.

I crossed my arms and pulled my t-shirt overhead. At least my underwear was lacy and sexier. I wasn't clueless after all.

He smirked, as his eyes danced over my body with need. He leaned forward, kissing the curve of each of my breasts.

"Fuck, you're the most beautiful woman I've ever laid eyes on." He reached around me and with the flick of his fingers on my bra strap, I felt it go slack. The straps fell off my shoulders before he hooked his fingers in them and pulled the bra away. He cupped my bare breasts, his hands covering them with ease. For my size, they weren't huge. I often joked that I'd been too busy growing my ass that I forgot about my tits. At least their smaller size allowed them to remain perky. Elle had informed me that was a bonus.

Rhys leaned forward and picked up his champagne glass to take a sip. He set the glass on the side table before taking my breast into his mouth.

The feel of the cool champagne on my warm skin made me gasp. As his tongue flicked and swirled at my nipple, I felt a drip run down my body, eliciting a shiver from me. Heat flared in my core. I resented the layers of clothing that still existed between us. He must have been feeling the same because he wrapped an arm around my waist and leaned me backward, lying me on the couch, before he hooked his fingers in my waistband and pulled away my leggings and panties. I was naked, with my legs spread, and I should have felt exposed while he admired me for a few moments. But I didn't. It felt right being this vulnerable with him. He ran a couple of fingers between my folds and pushed into my center. "You have the prettiest, pink pussy, baby girl. I can't believe it's all mine. That I'll be the first to experience you. I bet you feel fucking incredible."

I fisted the couch cushion as he played with my clit and worked his magic fingers around inside me, stimulating my most sensitive places. Venturing far deeper than he'd managed to in the alley. "There's—" I moaned. "—oh my, Rhys. There's only one way to find out."

He must have slipped another finger in me because I felt

fuller than I'd ever felt before as his fingers stretched at my walls. "You're so tight. How does that feel?"

"Amazing. I want more."

"Patience, baby girl, I've got more for you. But I've finally got you where I want you. Please, let me savor the moment. Let me worship your body with my mouth first."

I nodded as he slid down, hooking his free arm around my leg. The fingers on his other hand still filled me as he kissed a trail down my inner thigh before descending on my clit. He was gentle at first, then he surprised me with a rough suck. My body shuddered as I suppressed a moan.

I'd never had a man's mouth between my legs before. The feeling was so new, and I felt so vulnerable it bordered on too much. I ran my hand through Rhys's hair, anchoring myself to him. My body relaxed at the reminder that it was him I had between my legs.

"Don't hold back, baby. Let me know what feels good. Let me learn your body."

I looked down at him. He was staring up at me with his face half buried in me. It was too intense. I felt myself losing control under his gaze. The swell of my orgasm cresting. I pushed it away and shut my eyes.

He groaned and smacked at my ass. "Open your eyes."

My eyes shot open at his commanding tone.

"Good girl."

His praise ripped a loud moan from me.

"That's right baby, let Daddy know what your pussy likes."

Overcome with the intensity of his piercing gaze, I broke under the steady rhythm of his tongue and fingers. My cries of ecstasy filled the quiet space. If anyone was in the room next to us, they might've needed to cover their ears. No amount of soundproofing could have prevented adjoining rooms from hearing that. My face felt warm when the reality of what we'd just done sank in.

He pulled his fingers from me and licked them clean before sitting back with a satisfied grin on his face.

I sat up, reached for my glass of champagne, and took a sip.

He watched my every move without a word. There was something new about the way he regarded me. Like there was something under the surface that he was trying to keep contained.

I set down my glass. "Why do I feel like I'm not the only one that's been holding back?"

"We'll get to my specific tastes in due time. Tonight is all about you and making sure your first time is going down as it should."

I sighed. He was once again trying to protect my innocence. I didn't want it anymore. He could have it. How could I make that clear to him? I wanted him to make me his plaything when we were alone together. To take control. To unleash whatever beast he was keeping contained.

"What if I told you I want my first time to be memorable?"

He squinted at me. "In what way?"

I couldn't believe I was about to say it, but somehow, I knew the words he needed to hear most. "I want you to ruin me for other men, Daddy."

fifteen

RHYS

I reached out and grabbed her by the throat. Pulling her in for a rough kiss. Her eyes danced with excitement.

Fuck me.

"There's a lot more to you than what's on the surface, isn't there? My *nice* girl. My baby girl. All she wants is to be a bad girl for her daddy, doesn't she?"

She nodded, her eyes wide, but not with fear. She fucking wanted this. She wanted to be manhandled.

To have her pristine cunt ruined by my cock—by me.

She'd kept telling me she didn't want her innocence protected, but I wasn't hearing her. I thought she was just putting on a brave face.

"On your knees. You're going to gag on this cock before I fuck you with it and fill you. You still owe me from your little office tease the other day."

I slipped out of my lounge pants. My cock was harder than I'd seen it in decades. She slid off the couch and nestled herself between my legs.

Her eyes took in my size, an 'o' forming on her lips.

I took a fistful of her hair. Unwilling or unable to wait for her to come to me. "You'll have to open wider than that to fit me, my girl."

She parted her lips further, and I groaned as her hot, wet mouth took in the tip. Something overcame her at the first taste of me. Her hand wrapped around my shaft as she worked it. I pushed her down until I felt the muscles in her throat flex around my head. Then I backed off and let her do her thing. I just wanted to make sure she was well-acquainted. She'd played coy long enough. I leaned back and watched her head bob as she worked me hard. I groaned. She pulled back, looked up at me, and licked the full length of my shaft before kissing the tip and continuing.

"How did I not truly see you until this moment? The photos should have been my first hint that you're a dirty little slut underneath it all."

She reared back. "You—you saw them?"

"Of course, I did. Wasn't that the idea? If it wasn't, maybe you shouldn't have taken them on my phone."

"No, I mean yes, it was. It's just that you never mentioned them."

I shrugged. "Neither did you."

"True." She went back to sucking.

Mentioning the pictures had me thinking about the one where she'd hiked up her dress enough for me to see the curve of her ass-cheeks. How I'd fantasized about bending her over, her pussy popping out at me, and fucking her like that. That would have to wait, though. I wanted to watch her expressions while I fucked her for the first time. For two reasons. First, because it was hot-as-fuck, and second, because I wanted to make sure she was enjoying every moment.

"Get up."

"Do you not like it?"

"No, baby, I love it."

"But you didn't come."

"And I won't. I'm not wasting the load I have waiting for you in your mouth. It's going right into your hot little pussy. You okay with that?"

She nodded.

I patted my thigh. "Come sit on daddy's lap."

She straddled me. My bare cock slipped against her wetness. I maneuvered it to point at her opening as she lifted her hips, allowing her to take in the tip.

She gasped.

"Take it as slowly as you need."

She pursed her lips and narrowed her eyes at me. And slammed the rest of the way down.

"Fuck!" I groaned out as she collapsed against me. "Are you okay?"

"I'm not a porcelain doll, Rhys. I'm your 'little slut', remember?" Her cheeks flushed when she said it.

I shook my head and laughed. What had I gotten myself into?

She asked me to ruin her for other men, but if she kept it up, she was bound to ruin me for other women. Who was I kidding? She already had. She rocked her hips against me. It was a tight fit and I could tell she was feeling it too, despite how wet she was.

I took one of her perky tits in my mouth and felt a gush of slick heat envelop my cock. She was moving more, her big ass making a satisfying slapping noise against my thighs as I thrust into her deep. There was no containing her moans.

I stroked her hair. "That's a good girl. I love listening to you enjoy yourself." My lips met hers, smothering her whimpers of ecstasy with my mouth. I grabbed her ass cheeks, supporting her so she could bounce on my cock with ease. I'd have to fuck her in that another time. This woman was mine, and I was going to claim every hole she had as my own as often as I wanted.

I groaned into her mouth before grabbing a fistful of her hair and kissing down the side of her throat. Sucking hard on the pale flesh of her neck. I hadn't left a hickey on anyone since I was a teenager, but I wanted to mark this woman as my own in any and every way I could.

"Keep riding me that hard and I won't last long, baby."

She was panting now as I transferred my oral assault of her body from her neck to her breast. I sucked and pulled back to admire the faint purple mark left behind.

She started circling her hips. Shit. I dug my fingers into her meaty ass.

"I'm going to come in you, Paige. If you don't want that, you need to tell me now."

"Ugh! Come on, Daddy. Fill me," she cried out.

Fuck!

My cock spasmed, spilling pump after pump of my hot seed into her young fertile pussy.

I hugged her tight to my chest.

Her breathing was heavy as I stroked her back.

What had she done to me? We'd only known each other a week, and I'd already do anything for her.

She was mine now. Company policy be fucking damned. From that moment forward, it didn't apply to us. Being the boss had to come with some perks. Paige was my woman and people would have to deal with that come Monday morning.

Was it unfair?

Sure, it was.

Did I care?

Not one fucking bit.

sixteen

PAIGE

Nerves bubbled in my stomach as Rhys and I made our way up the elevator to the office hand-in-hand Monday morning. I moved my bags to Rhys's hotel suite over the weekend, and we spent the rest of the time in New York in meetings, taking pictures, and exploring the food trucks. When we weren't in the hotel room having sex, of course. The client was happy. We were happy.

The trip couldn't have gone any better than it had.

Getting home to my bed was a bit of relief, though. Rhys and I were both relentless in the bedroom and my body was aching for the best of reasons. But I wasn't used to him yet. He'd insisted on picking me up to commute together.

He assured me we were in it together. A switch had flipped. The man who talked about keeping us a secret or about how we might not make things work was gone in an instant. He'd been replaced by a self-assured man. A man who knew what he wanted and went for it, the one he spoke of the night we met.

"Are you sure this is a good idea? Going public so soon?"

He smirked. "Beats sneaking around, doesn't it?"

"I don't know about that. Sneaking around could be fun."

"Would you rather we keep things between us for now?"

Rather? No, of course not.

But did it seem like the wiser idea? Yes. I nodded.

"Okay, baby, it's up to you. When you're ready, I'm ready."

I stood up on my tiptoes and gave him a quick kiss.

"Come back here, you tease. If I have to tolerate a whole day of working around you without being able to touch you, then I'm going to need a better kiss than that."

I laughed as he pulled me to him, resting my hand on his chest, as he kissed me deeper.

The elevator doors slid open, and I heard an audible gasp. We both turned our heads to see who'd caught us.

Roxy.

Her jaw was slack as she shook her head at us. "I knew it."

So much for keeping things a secret.

Rhys stepped out of the elevator, unfazed. "Coming, Paige?" He extended his hand.

"No, I'll be back soon."

Roxanne stepped into the elevator next to me, pressing the button for the lobby. She wouldn't even look over at me.

"It's not what you think."

"So, you didn't lie to me?"

"No, well, not exactly."

She shot me a look. "Come on. I'm not an idiot, and

don't pretend like I didn't just witness you kissing the boss."

"Of course, you did. But I can explain."

"No explanation necessary. He hired his girlfriend. Nice effort trying to pile all that extra work on you to make it look like he wasn't playing favorites."

"Stop! It isn't like that. He and I met before we knew I was working for him. The weekend I arrived in Seattle, I went out with my friend. He was at the bar we went to, and we spent the evening together. I didn't expect to see him on Monday morning."

She rolled her eyes. "Right."

"I'm telling you the truth."

She turned to me and put her hand on her hip. "Fine, you're telling me your version of the truth. I believe you, Paige."

"My 'version of the truth' *is* the truth."

She sighed. "I know his type, is all."

"His type?"

It was clear she had the wrong impression of Rhys.

"A man who exploits his power to get younger women. Look, we don't know each other well, but I can tell you're sweet. I just don't want you to get too wrapped up in whatever fantasy he's feeding you."

"You've misjudged him."

"You *hope* I have."

"Rhys isn't like that."

She stepped out of the elevator, and I followed her into the lobby. "Where are you going anyhow?"

"Martin asked me if I could 'be a doll' and fetch coffee for the investor meeting."

"Gross."

"Right? Well, that *gross* man is your boyfriend's best friend. Did you know that?"

"No, but—"

"Then maybe you don't know as much about Mr. Lockwood as you think you do."

"Do you?"

"No, let's just call it a hunch."

More like jumping to conclusions. My best friend and I were total opposites. Martin and Rhys being close meant nothing at all.

I walked through the lobby with her. "Well, I'll tell you the same thing I told him when he said he was worried I'd get hurt."

"He told you that?"

"Yes, he was concerned about going any further with me because he didn't want to hurt me if we couldn't be together. But I know the risks and it doesn't make me want him, or us, any less."

She pursed her lips. "Paige, come on, he's even told you he's going to hurt you and you're still going through with it? Look, I get it. He's handsome, successful, charming, and wealthy. And for girls like us, girls that are just trying to scrape by, it seems like a chance at living the dream. But that's all it is. A dream."

Girls like us?

"I'm not after his money."

I didn't need his money. My father would give me anything I asked if I wanted to take it. That's not what I wanted. Did my being with Rhys give off that impression? Is that what people would think? Of course.

I'd thought the same about plenty of my dad's ex-girlfriends. That wasn't right of me. I felt sick to my stomach.

"It's sinking in now, isn't it?"

"No. Not in the way you're thinking."

"What do you mean?"

"I don't need Rhys's money. I've got plenty of money at my disposal. My father's Horace Stanley."

"Wait, what? The celebrity chef?"

I smacked my lips. "Yup. So, what's sinking in is that I've been guilty of judging women who've tried to date my father in the same way you're judging me. And it's not right. As a woman who claims to be committed to social justice and women's rights, you of all people should be ashamed of yourself. Because I sure am. You've put me on the receiving end. You're acting like I'm incapable of seeing the situation for what it is. You're right about one thing though, you don't know me. And guess what? You don't know him either."

I was through trying to convince her that my feelings for Rhys were genuine and that I was enough for him. Enough to be deserving of the honest feelings of a successful man. I spun on my heels.

"Wait, Paige, I'm—"

"You're what? You've said enough." I shrugged. "Just stay out of it. You don't have to believe in us, but I do. Just leave us be. If you have any respect for me at all, forget what you saw."

I didn't wait for her reply. It didn't matter anymore. She'd do what she wanted. I stormed back upstairs. Rhys needed to know about my conversation with Roxy. I bypassed Naomi's desk and went right to his office. Knocking on the door. There was no answer.

"He has a meeting in the boardroom."

Right, the investor's meeting.

I turned and Naomi tipped her head at me.

I paced and threw up my hands. "Can you tell him I came by? That I need to talk to him as soon as possible?"

"If you have concerns about your position, you can speak with your department head about them."

I was tired of people trying to gatekeep me. "Then tell him his *girlfriend* came by, will you?"

I watched the shock register as her face fell. Well, he wanted us to be public.

For better or worse.

We were public.

seventeen

RHYS

By Tuesday morning, the media circus hit. And by the afternoon, Paige went into hiding at her father's insistence. A forbidden relationship between Horace Stanley's youngest daughter and one of Seattle's most eligible bachelors who also happened to be twenty-two years her senior was too good of a story for the press to pass up.

I'd given the office the day off, except for Naomi and Martin. We needed to seal up the office and do damage control.

"Hold my calls today, Naomi."

"Yes, Mr. Lockwood."

Martin followed me into my office.

I pulled a bottle of scotch out of my desk drawer and cracked it. It was a gift from a client. I didn't drink while at work, but I was making an exception. I poured Martin a drink.

He took the glass from me. "You've got it bad for this one, don't you?"

I groaned. "You ever want something so fucking bad that even when you know you can't have it, you still can't talk yourself out of it?"

"I kind of figured you had something going on with Paige."

I nodded. "How did you know?"

"I caught you two eyeing each other the day the fire alarm went off. Not to mention you both showed up late and within a minute of each other. Doesn't take a genius to put two-and-two together."

I rolled my head back and let out a puff of air. "Here, I thought I was being clever."

"What the hell happened? Who blew the top off this whole thing?"

"Roxanne Westwood. Serves me right for hiring an online social justice seeker. But I didn't expect to become her next target. Before Paige, there wasn't any dirt on me. I thought I was safe." The girl's reputation preceded her, that's for sure. It's the reason I hired her. But I wasn't looking to have the weapon of mass destruction that was her social media following, turned on me.

"Are you sure it was her?"

"She caught Paige and me kissing in the elevator yesterday. The two of them had it out. I'm as sure as I'll ever be."

"I thought maybe it was a scorned woman. One that figured that if you ever broke your policy, it'd be with her." He tipped his head toward the glass wall that separated me from Naomi's desk.

"Naomi? No, she wouldn't do anything like that."

"Love will make you do funny things, Rhys. Just look at the situation you're in now."

It was true. What I was doing with Paige was out of the norm for me, but I was hard-pressed to regret it. "Keyword, there was love. Naomi's my assistant. If she's in love with me, she's never shown it."

"Unless you count the decade of long hours and doting on your every need."

"Pretty sure that's in her job description."

"Keep telling yourself that. But you seem convinced it's this Roxy chick anyhow." Martin shook his head. "The press is going wild."

I swirled my scotch and took a sip. It was fucking awful stuff, but the burn felt nice. "I know."

He shrugged. "What's the big deal, though? They're acting like you're the first older man to hook up with a young woman. It's not that rare. It'll blow over soon enough.

"Maybe so, but she's also my employee. Don't you think that poses a bit of an ethical dilemma? It's not a line I ever imagined myself crossing."

"I don't think you ever imagined yourself with any woman except for Katrina. But it's been twenty years. It was about time you let yourself be happy again."

"What makes you think I haven't been happy? I've built my company from the ground up. It's now the single most successful firm in the nation. I'd say I'm pretty darn happy."

"Wow, I know you're stubborn, but I never thought you were delusional. You're confusing happiness with wealth. What you've done with Velocity has been amazing. I'm honored to be a part of it and that you took me along for the ride. But I've known you for almost thirty years and that's long enough to know that you're long overdue for someone like her to come into your life."

"True. I'm just not sure how to make it right. The sooner I can get this situation under control, the sooner I can get things back to normal around here. I need to fix this —fast. But how?"

Figuring it out meant Paige would return to me. At least, I hoped. That's assuming she even wanted to after this. She looked mortified when she saw the article outlining our affair and the pictures of us in New York.

Wait just a fucking minute.

We were being followed over the weekend? I was so ready to pin this all on Roxanne, that I hadn't stopped to think until that moment. Then again, Paige had said she caught on to us from that first day in the office.

"It's not my place to tell you what to do. That's up to you to decide. You need to do what feels right. Remember when we said we'd always trust our gut instincts? It hasn't failed us yet, has it? What's your gut telling you to do? Just go with it."

I lifted the glass to my lips and thought about what he said. I had always trusted my gut, and I knew the moment I met her, that she was the one for me. Even with this fucked up situation, I knew she still was. Maybe it was wrong of me to pursue her, but none of that mattered now. The only thing that mattered was the fact that I couldn't lose her.

"Those gears are turning way too hard, buddy. That's not trusting your gut. Why don't you just join her in hiding? Let me run the show around here for a little while before the dust settles."

That was an idea. Then again, the way Martin mishandled his own money meant he'd probably bankrupt my business before the media was on to the next scandal.

No, I had to face this head-on.

"I just need to sort it out. The press has been hounding me for interviews all day."

Maybe I needed a platform to make my feelings and

intentions for Paige known. It was better than the media coming to inaccurate conclusions about what was going on between us. Then again, they could've twisted things. It could've backfired. But I had to take that risk.

I buzzed through to Naomi's desk. "Inform the local stations that I'll be holding a press conference in an hour. They want answers. I'll give them the truth."

"Mr. Lockwood—"

I hung up before she could try to change my mind.

It was time to fight fire with fire.

Roxanne may have had social media at her disposal, but I had every major news station at mine. She told her version of the story.

It was time for me to tell mine.

eighteen

RHYS

The cameras flashed as I took the podium. My phone buzzed. I picked it up to read the text message.

PAIGE

I miss you.

It won't be long now, my girl.

I shoved my phone into my pocket and narrowed my eyes at the rows of reporters hungry for a story. They'd turned the most beautiful thing I'd ever encountered into tabloid fodder.

Didn't they have better things to do than harass us? But the answer to that was no. Paige was Horace Stanley's daughter and famous by association. She was also an heiress to his ever-growing luxury hotel chain. How she'd managed to stay out of the limelight for as long as she had was the true mystery.

I was popular in my own right, too. I'd been named Seattle's most eligible bachelor more times than I could count. Okay, more times than I cared about. They'd just about given up on me dating someone, and then I popped up involved with a woman half my age who also happened to be my employee. It would be the first and the last time I addressed the issue publicly.

The reporters started firing questions. A jumble of words cast out in my direction. There was only one question that stood out among them because it infuriated me.

"Do you regret your actions?"

I grit my teeth. "Enough!"

The roar of the crowd dulled to a chatter. I glanced over, spotting Roxanne in the back corner, her arms folded across her chest.

She had a lot of nerve showing up.

But I guess she couldn't miss out on her handy work.

I cleared my throat, and the mic squealed with feedback. "My actions weren't ideal. You're all right to have questions, but this is not the simple case of misconduct it's being portrayed as. At no point was I out to take advantage of Ms. Stanley, nor was she hoping to take advantage of me. We'd met each other before we even realized she worked for Velocity. Once we found out about the unfortunate situation we were in, we tried to avoid taking things any further. But the lure of one another was too strong. What we shared —share—is an honest and reciprocal relationship. So, if you're here looking for a scandal, or looking to make me some poster boy for evil CEOs, move along. I don't regret a single moment I've spent with Paige."

The crowd erupted with questions again. I pointed to a young, bright-eyed reporter in the front row. "Mr. Lockwood, do you love her?"

Only since the moment I'd laid eyes on her.

"I do, very much."

The reporter next to her chimed in. "Where is Ms. Stanley now?"

My heart was in my throat thinking about Paige alone, dealing with the aftermath of this situation on her own. At least she was away from the onslaught of the press. Her father saw to that. But she was alone, and that bugged the fuck out of me. I should have been by her side and not dealing with these assholes but they needed to be dealt with.

"I'm not sure, but Paige, if you're watching this, I love you. You stumbled into my world, and I have loved you ever since. And I have something I need to ask you."

"What do you want to ask her?" A voice yelled out from the back corner. I looked over, realizing it was Roxanne's.

"That's between her and me."

Roxanne pursed her lips. She pulled her phone from her pocket and spun on her heels out of the room.

Questions continued as I watched Roxanne slip through the doors.

I jumped off the podium and ripped the mic from my shirt, discarding it on the floor.

"Press conference over," I said, and the sea of people parted as I charged my way through them.

The crowd was hot on my heels when I caught up with her.

"Roxanne, wait."

She turned around. "Mr. Lockwood."

"Are you happy with yourself?"

She shook her head. "Happy? I'm here because I thought Paige might be here. I wanted to tell her that I'm sorry."

"That's not good enough after what you've done. You

betrayed her trust and invited this chaos into our lives." I pointed back at the room full of reporters.

Roxy put a hand on her hip. "You think I did this? I didn't do this."

"There's no sense in denying it."

"I—I'm not. What I wanted to tell Paige was that I'm sorry for jumping to conclusions. She didn't deserve that. And hearing you speak about her, you didn't either. So, I'm sorry."

"You weren't the one who involved the media, were you?"

She threw up her hands. "That's what I'm telling you. Paige said she didn't want anyone else to know. She protected my identity when asked. It was only fair that I keep her secret too. Besides, it was the right thing to do. You're not the only one that wants to protect her, you know? Heck, I've only known the girl a week and I can already tell she's one of the most genuine people I've ever met."

"You're right about that."

She gave me a slight smile. "Tell her I owe her a spa day or something like that once this is all over, okay?"

I nodded. "You got it."

I returned to the office. If Roxy wasn't responsible, I needed to figure out who was. "Naomi, we need to speak in my office. Now."

"Have a seat." I pointed to the chair across from where I sat before rounding my desk to take a seat.

"Let's get right down to it, shall we?"

"Is something wrong, Mr. Lockwood?"

I took a deep breath. "Did you have us followed in New York?"

"What? No. Why would I do a thing like that?"

"Did you know about Paige and me before yesterday?"

"No. Why?" She glanced at the door to my office.

"Because there were only so many people that knew we were alone in New York together. Martin said you may harbor feelings for me. So, I'll ask again. Did you know about Paige and me before yesterday?"

"Martin said that?"

"Yes, he did. Answer the question."

She sighed, "Yes, I knew about you and Paige."

"How did you know?"

"The pictures on your phone. I was in the company cloud retrieving some photos for Martin and I saw them—we saw them."

"How long ago was this?"

"The day she started here."

"You've known from the very beginning? Did you have me followed?"

"No, well, sort of. But I swear I never meant for those photos to get into the wrong hands. Martin said we needed to know what was going on. That you'd lose your head over this woman, and we needed to be prepared. You've been a lonely man for a long time—"

"Fucker." I'd worried about him making a play for my company in the beginning, but as the years passed, I'd become complacent.

"He said I should have you followed so we could deal with the situation. That we were only doing it to know what we were up against."

"If you didn't intend for the photos to get in the hands

of the media, how did they end up there? Did you send them?"

She shook her head. "I'd never do that. I love my job. As far as I knew, they were deleted. Marty must have kept copies. You're the best boss I've ever had. It's just you and I have something in common."

"What's that?"

"We'll do anything for the one we love."

"And you're in love with me?"

She chuckled. "No."

"If not me, then who?"

"Martin. You aren't the only one capable of breaking company policy."

They were involved?

Come to think of it, I hadn't seen him picking up any women as of late. And he used to do it every time we went out.

"You're in love with Martin?"

"I am."

"We've been a team for decades. I know he has his issues, but I thought I could trust him."

"No, you were a team many years *ago*." Tears were welling in her eyes. "He's been your employee ever since. All these years and you never thought to make him a partner. It hurts him."

"And I never will. He's a heck of a project manager, Naomi, but he's got a pretty bad gambling habit."

"He does?"

I nodded.

"I'm sorry, Mr. Lockwood, I never would have listened to him had I known he was endangering the company. Why would he do this?" The tears were flowing now. Her shoulders shook as she sobbed into her hands. "I can't lose this job."

"A gambler doesn't need any motivation other than money, or lack of money to get resourceful—or deceitful."

The deep betrayal I felt knowing both of my most trusted employees had conspired against me made me wish even more that Paige was by my side.

I looked up at the woman crying before me. Love had once again threatened to derail my company, but could I blame her?

"Stop, Naomi, it's okay. Call security and have Martin removed from the premises."

I'd known the guy for thirty years, but he'd lied to my face earlier and plotted against me. He'd used this poor woman to get at me. There was no point in rehashing things and allowing him to lie some more. "I believe your intentions were good, Naomi, but you'll have to promise me you'll have nothing to do with him if I keep you on here."

"I promise."

"Good, because I'm going to need you to hold things down here for a few days."

I had to go make sure the woman I loved was okay.

nineteen

PAIGE

"Everything's going to be okay," Elle told me over video chat.

"We just made things official. We hadn't even settled into our new relationship. I'm afraid that all of this happening so soon is going to make him think twice about whether we're meant to be."

"I think you two are going to be just fine."

"Look, I appreciate your confidence in us, but how can you be so sure?"

"Just call it a hunch. Anyway, I can't be late for class. You should see my professor. He's stunning."

"I bet he is. If he's motivating you to show up to class on time."

She laughed. "Shut it. I have a newfound appreciation for my education, okay? And he looks like he has a thing-or-two that he could teach me outside the classroom."

"You're in your final year. Don't get yourself expelled."

"Where's the fun in that? Imagine the story we could

tell our kids. Daddy and mommy both work at Burger Shack because we threw away our careers when we couldn't keep our hands off each other. It's romantic!"

I laughed. She always had a way of lightening my mood. Even when I was stuck in a secluded cabin in the mountains of Oregon. We said our goodbyes, and I made my way out to the deck.

I should have felt at home with the earthy smell of the outdoors in my nostrils and the sunset peeking through the evergreens. The forests of Oregon were where I'd spent a good portion of my youth. But it was hard to feel at home when I was all alone, apart from my dad's security team. Though I appreciated them guarding the house and bringing me supplies.

Still, I was missing a very key ingredient that would make this trip more agreeable.

An ingredient that was a surefire way to make me feel at home.

Rhys.

I sighed into the breeze, sending a wish into the universe that we'd be okay.

Somehow this wouldn't be the end of us. Rhys was the best thing that had ever happened to me and everything I'd been looking for in a partner.

"Could you have been any harder to find?"

My skin tingled as the familiar gravel tone of Rhys's voice enveloped me. I spun around. "You're here. How did you find me?"

"Elle. Our matchmaker struck again. I sent her a message, and she was more than happy to give away your top-secret locale. I don't know about that girl, but I like her." Rhys stood by the sliding glass door, shaking his head and laughing. He looked so inviting in his dark green cashmere sweater and gray slacks. I crossed the deck to his open arms, and he wrapped me in them.

He'd come for me. Amid everything, he'd chosen to be by my side. I pressed my cheek to his muscular chest and squeezed him. "I was so worried."

"It's just press, Paige. Nothing I can't handle." He stroked my hair.

"Do you think they'll leave us alone already?"

"Not a chance. Which is why I've come here to be with you. I'll set up a remote office until things die down."

"You'd do that for me?"

He curled a finger under my chin, tipping my head back. "I'd do anything for you, baby girl. Don't you realize that?"

"I do—it's just—I worried that experiencing complications so soon would rock our foundation. I should have known."

He pressed a kiss to my forehead. "There's nothing and no one that can change how I feel about you. I've waited too long to find you. I knew from the moment I laid eyes on you that you were an important part of my world. And *now* you're my world."

I exhaled as relief washed over me. There I was, feeling worried things would get worse and somehow the entire experience had only brought us closer.

"There's something I need to tell you, Paige."

My heart seized in my chest. I couldn't speak out of fear that the next words to come out of his mouth would somehow shatter everything.

"I don't know why I've even waited this long. But from the moment we met, I started falling for you. Even though we haven't known each other long. And we still have so much to learn about one another. You're a bright light in a dark world, baby girl. You're the beacon that brought my heart out of seclusion. And what you must know above all else is that I love you, Paige. I've loved every moment we've spent together, and I can't wait to spend many more with you. What's left of my life, if you'll allow me to."

A smile overtook my face before I threw my arms around his neck and kissed him. "I love you too, Rhys. There hasn't been a single second when I haven't wanted you—or us. You've shifted my perspective on love and relationships in such a short time. All the things that I never could find interest in with others, I find myself desperate to have with you. It just feels natural. Somehow, you looked past my often shy and awkward exterior to find the real me."

"A wise woman once told me we should make the most of the time we've been given. Do you think it still counts when we won't settle for anything less than forever?"

"Even more so."

He kneeled on one knee and pulled a little box from his pocket. "They want something to talk about, so let's give them something to talk about." He opened the box, and a brilliant pink solitaire set in a stunning platinum band stared back at me.

"Rhys, it's gorgeous." My hand trembled as I reached out to touch his.

"No, you're gorgeous and precious and rare. This pink diamond is almost as rare as you are. I chose it because the color reminded me of the bubblegum I gave you that first night, and I've known since then that I was stuck on you. And if you're feeling the same, marry me."

I'd never thought much about what my wedding ring might look like someday. It was stunning and the reason behind it was perfect. But it was the man on one knee that made it all feel right.

"Yes, of course, I'll marry you."

He slipped the ring on my finger and swept me off my feet, carrying me back into the cabin. "Aren't you supposed to wait until the wedding night to carry me across the threshold?"

"For you, my love, I'll break every tradition and boundary. Now, point me toward the bedroom. We have some celebrating to do."

I pointed down the hall, my eyes never leaving his face. As I took in the angles of his jaw, his stubbled chin with gray hair sprinkled throughout, I was thankful for every risk, every stolen kiss, and every moment I'd shared with this man.

Through misconduct, I'd met my match.

epilogue

RHYS

ONE YEAR LATER

A rap sounded out on my office door. I knew that knock.

"Come in."

Paige, my stunning wife, stepped into the room and clicked the door closed behind her. "I was wondering if you were interested in an early lunch?"

I raised my brow. 'Early lunch' was our code for fooling around in the office, but things had been so busy at Velocity we hadn't had the time in a few months. Roxy and Naomi continued to work for us. Paige had accepted Roxy's apology and the two had become very close. She'd even been a bridesmaid at our wedding.

Martin owned up to what he'd done and had been to treatment. He admitted that he'd convinced the photographer to quit and had concocted the entire plan for Paige and me to be alone in New York. I didn't know whether to thank the fucker or punch him since it had been the turning point in my relationship with my wife.

Still, I hadn't invited him to return to Velocity and he hadn't asked. Did it mean he wouldn't attempt something like it again? I didn't know, but I'd agreed to be friends again with Paige's blessing. I just kept him on a need-to-know basis.

He was lucky I had the most stunning and forgiving wife in the world.

Paige leaned her back against the door. "I'm starving. Feed me?"

She was also the most insatiable.

"Lock the door."

I stood unbuckling my belt. She didn't have to ask me twice. The way she was filling out her pleated skirt was all the convincing I needed. She had her hair up in a ponytail and she wore a tight white button-up shirt tucked into her skirt. She was looking more like a naughty schoolgirl than a marketing executive, but I wasn't about to complain. "To what do I owe this occasion?"

She ran her finger along the front of my desk. "Wouldn't you like to know..." She paused, turned, and leaned over my desk. "Daddy."

I rounded the desk in a flash and pushed her down. "I can see I'm going to need to fuck whatever it is out of you."

She giggled. "You're welcome to try."

I grabbed her ponytail, leaned over her, and gave her a messy kiss. She moaned into my mouth. "I haven't failed yet, baby girl."

"I know you haven't, but you might this time."

This was my once shy girl. She was still a good girl for any outsider looking in. But as the year passed, she opened up more to me in private, her bratty side coming through. Her brave words, nor mine, no longer turned her cheeks rosy. And my cock was all that much harder for it.

I flipped up her skirt and pulled down her black tights and panties, revealing her full, bare ass. Her pussy popped through her thick thighs, much in the way I'd always imagined it would. I slipped two fingers along her seam and plunged them in, before pulling them away to slap her ass, eliciting a moan from her. "Are you ready to tell me now?"

"Nope."

"Fine, then you've asked for it. Remember this when you can't sit tonight."

"Oooh, I'm so scared."

I rolled my lips inward, biting down on them to prevent myself from chuckling at her insubordination.

She was just too fucking cute. It drove me wild. I pulled my belt from my pants and folded it. She knew the sound and squirmed in my grip. I tapped her ass with the belt as a warning. "Change your mind yet?"

I pulled my cock from my slacks, stroking it a few times, before slapping her ass with the belt. A crack echoed through the room, and she grunted out a moan.

"Shh, Daddy, they're going to hear you."

"You're wrong, my girl, they're going to hear *you*. Because if you keep this up, I'm going to spank you hard until you scream."

I rubbed at the red mark on her behind, before I grabbed her wrists and held them against her back, her upper body flush with my desk. She needed to know who was in control. I discarded the belt and positioned the tip of my cock at her entrance. We'd been trying for some time to conceive. I'd been filling her as often as we could manage. I smeared my pre-cum around the opening before slamming into her. She cried out. Naomi was at lunch, or I'm sure she would have heard that one.

I pumped in and out of her hard and fast. Her tight pussy was slick around me. I could never get enough of this woman. I let go of her arms and ran my hand over her ass, giving it another slap. Pulled my dick from her and smeared her puckered opening with our mixed juices. And massaged them in with my thumb.

She moaned. "Oh no, Daddy, not there."

It was tempting to take her ass, like I'd done before, to show her who was in charge. But she needed to be lubed up for that, and neither of us came prepared. I slipped my dick back inside her and popped my thumb in her ass instead. She squirmed some, but as I worked both holes, she relaxed into it and her moans became more frequent.

I reached around her and found her clit, massaging it. My balls tightened as I felt her clamp down on me. She was close. Fuck, so was I. It wouldn't be long until I'd have her crying out in ecstasy.

"I'm going to come," she panted.

I pulled back from her. Leaving her hanging. "Nope, if you want your release, you need to tell me what's going on.

She whimpered. "No, don't stop now. Please, please, let me come and I'll tell you everything."

"Hmm, that's not how it works, and you know it."

"Just this once, please."

"You promise you'll be a good girl and tell me right after?"

"I promise."

"If you're not being truthful, I'm canceling my meetings, and you'll be spending the rest of the day under my desk sucking my cock and doing whatever else I desire. I won't let you come again. Not until I say so. Understood?"

She laughed. "Are you threatening me with a good time?"

"Paige," I warned. "Be a good girl."

"I'm going to tell you. I promise, okay?"

"Okay, you'd better." I found her clit again and thrust back into her. Her excitement hadn't faded despite my interlude. It couldn't have been more than a minute later when I felt her clamp down and cum on my cock. It was so fucking hot listening to her unleash beneath me, it pushed me over the edge, forcing me to pump spurt-after-spurt of hot cum inside her.

When we were done, we cleaned up as best we could, and I pulled her into my lap.

I kissed her. "Now, what did you have to tell me?"

She bit her lip. It had to be something big. I hadn't seen her nervous around me in quite some time. "In eight months, you're not only going to be my daddy in the bedroom, but you're going to be a dad for real."

"Are you... fuck, are you saying that we did it?" No wonder she said I couldn't fuck it out of her. My seed was planted in her womb. I chuckled. Clever girl.

She nodded, a broad smile on her face. "Yes," she squealed.

I squeezed her in my arms and kissed her. If someone had told me that after over twenty years of being alone, I'd find love again or that I'd have the family I'd sought and failed to build decades before, I'd have laughed them off. But this incredible woman had given me all of that and more.

Our love was proof that some rules were meant to be broken.

Thank you for reading, and I hope you enjoyed Paige and Rhys's story.

Are you craving more forbidden age-gap romances? Elle's story, Miss Education, is up next. Keep up with the couples of the Man on a Mission series, updates, future releases, and giveaways, by joining me at:
https://sendfox.com/literarylovepotions

Endless Love,

Lia

miss education

CHAPTER ONE

ELLE

I sprinkled more pink confetti over the desk and stepped back to look at the damage.

Helium balloons. *Check.*

Plastic pink flamingos. *Check.*

An obscene amount of glitter? *Double check.*

I perched a sign on the desk that read 'Are you ready to get flocked?'

It was smaller than I wanted, but I had the added challenge of sneaking it into a college unnoticed. So while I may have wanted a billboard, I'd have to settle for standard letter size. I tipped my head at it. It was glittery enough, but the flamingo clip art I'd tossed on it could have used a bit more thought.

Oh well, it would do.

The obnoxious amount of glitter and confetti to top it all off was the cherry on top of my office mess. He'd be finding it in places all semester long. Then again, after we defiled his new office together, so would I.

Glitter, after all, is the gift that keeps giving. Especially once it finds its way into your nether regions, in my experience.

I surveyed the room one last time with my hands perched on my hips like I was Christopher Columbus, surveying the magnificence of his latest land discovery. Except mine was less majestic and much... tackier.

I could have squealed. It was so—perfect.

Nate would be here any minute, but I couldn't think of a better way to celebrate his new teaching position with Brooks College than to make a total mess of his office.

There was only one thing left to do.

I slipped off my black trench coat, revealing the school-girl outfit I'd sewn for this little one-on-one celebration. My family had not only founded the college but still ran it to this day. Nate and I weren't an item, but as my boy bestie, he'd been around enough for my father to take a shine to him and he benefitted from riding the coattails of my nepotism. Even still, we were just two friends that had taken to fooling around while single.

And I was *always* single.

We'd known each other for eleven years, ever since his family moved to Oregon. When I set down my coat on the back of the chair, a gust of air knocked over the sign and I bent over the desk to reach across it and set it back right.

A throat cleared behind me. "What have you done to my office?"

I froze, but the lilt of the possessor's deep Irish accent was my first hint that it wasn't Nate, the all-American west coast boy, standing behind me at that very moment. Nor was it him that just had a full-on view of the ass cheeks that peeked out from the bottom of my ridiculously short skirt.

Yup, in hindsight, I should have waited for Nate to arrive to reveal my outfit.

Too late for that now, I thought as I turned to see who my surprise voyeur was.

I sucked in a breath the moment my eyes locked on him. His hair was jet black, with a streak of silver that was almost white shooting out from his widow's peak. His belt buckle flashed in menace at me under the fluorescent lights, drawing my eyes down. The way he filled out his black slacks was criminal. He'd paired them with a white button-up shirt with a couple of buttons undone at the collar.

He eyed me up and down. "The school uniforms sure are different in America." He brushed past me and set his distressed, brown leather briefcase down on the desk. "But given your media, I'm not surprised."

When I realized I'd just been standing there with my nipples on full display under the sheer mesh tie top, I dove for my trench and pulled it on, tying it closed with a double knot.

This man had seen much more than the PG version of me. When I designed the pattern for the top, I'd made it sexy but well-supported, so at least it wasn't a terrible show to tune in to.

He wasn't the first, nor was he likely to be the last, to see parts of me bare, but still I wanted to run for the hills. But that wasn't my style, so instead, I extended my hand to him. "Elle Brooks. And you are?"

His eyes were cold and his face expressionless, yet it still reeked of disappointment as he stared at me and my offered hand.

Fine, don't introduce yourself.

"Which room were you looking for? Because this is Nate Baldwin's office."

He stared down at my hand and let out a little disapproving rumble in his throat before folding his arms across his chest. "He resigned."

Resigned?

I shook my head. "You must be mistaken Mr—?"

"Professor," he corrected me. "Professor Byrne."

"Well, *Professor* Byrne, you must be mistaken because I just spoke with Nate last week and he said that—"

He threw his hands up. "Or maybe they fired him for entertaining naked women in his office," he said, before shrugging. "Who knows, Ms. Brooks, but the fact remains, you're the one that's mistaken."

Heat flared between my thighs at the way he said my name and it wasn't just the accent, it was the fluctuation in his tone when he said it. My name was a sin on his lips. Or was it a promise of sins to come? I couldn't be too sure, but I could listen to him say it all day on repeat and never tire of it.

He snapped his lips shut and growled at me. Maybe I'd read too many shifter romances, but I half expected him to turn into some feral beast on command. His glare turned more and more glowering the longer I stood there in silence.

What had he said? Oh right!

"Hey, that's not a fair statement. I'm not naked. Am I underdressed for the occasion? Yes. But I'm at least half-dressed."

He did a double-take. "However you want to put it. It left little to the imagination."

Did this guy have any idea how sexy he was? His body

was so hard it looked like they cut it from marble. Whoever 'they' were, I wanted to thank them. He was a true Adonis. Even his chilly demeanor was five-alarm pants fire-inducing.

He picked up the sign. "What does 'get flocked' mean?"

"It's a play on words. Like a flock of flamingos." I pointed at the three hard pink plastic birds propped up along the bookshelf. "And get fuc—"

He raised his hand to stop me. "Say no more. I get it."

He gave me a slow nod, rounded his desk and sat down behind it, his eyes dropping to the desktop. He swiped some confetti and glitter aside and, without looking up, asked, "Do you work here?"

"No, I'm a student."

His posture went rigid. How he hadn't connected my last name and the fact that we were at *Brooks* College, I wasn't sure.

Gee, Elle, do you think maybe your peep show distracted him?

But not only had my family founded the school generations ago, but my father was the president of the college board of directors. It afforded me some liberties around campus and I enjoyed taking them.

This miscalculation was making me feel bad, though.

I brushed some glitter into my palm. "Let me clean up my mess. I'm sorry, by the way. "

He shook his head. "No. Just go."

"But the glitter—"

"Look, the last thing I need is a student that called her former professor by his first name and felt comfortable enough to show up naked—"

"Mostly naked," I corrected him

He pinched the bridge of his nose and sucked in a long

breath. "*Mostly* naked. Anyway, the bottom line is you have to go. I don't want anyone to spot you in here. You're not very careful. I don't need to be presumed guilty by association."

He swiped at his desk some more, sending a cascade of glitter over the edge before shaking his head some again. "I'll clean it up later. I have a class."

He stood, ushering me toward the door like he was a rancher and I was some stubborn cow that refused to make her way into the corral. Or were corrals for horses? Who knew? I didn't speak cowboy. Professor Byrne didn't look like the ranching type either, or I would have asked.

He had the wrong impression of me, well not completely, but Nate had been around so long that he was an honorary family member. My father had even extended his reach to include him. He wasn't just some professor that I was messing around with or whatever this guy was thinking. I opened my mouth to protest, but before I could, the heavy oak door slammed shut in my face as I stood in the hall, stunned and maybe a little concerned.

It was looking like the only person I'd managed to 'flock' was myself. Either that, or today was the beginning of the best semester ever.

CHAPTER TWO

FINN

The chalk cracked between my fingertips at the sound of her laughter.

I didn't know if she was trying to fuck with me because of our encounter in the morning. But that was what was happening.

I looked over my shoulder and her eyes flicked in my direction before a subtle smile grew on her lips.

She knew what she was doing all right.

Brat.

Under any other circumstances, I'd tame her wild ways. But professional decorum prevented me.

I spun. "What if I told you all there was a one-ton gold nugget buried under that tree out there?" I pointed at the window toward the willow tree. "How much is it worth?"

Someone raised their hand. "Current market value?"

Elle pulled out her phone and was tapping away at the screen.

I forced myself to look away and ignore her. "Anyone else?"

"Upwards of fifty million?" another student called out.

"That's the same answer, only more defined thanks to Google. But it's still wrong."

Elle peeked up from her phone at me and rolled in her lips, biting down on them.

"Do you have something to offer to the conversation, Ms. Brooks?"

She set her phone down. "Sorry, I wasn't paying attention, but I'm all ears now. What's up?"

Lies. Pure fucking lies.

But I indulged her. "What's *up* is we were discussing the value of the one-ton gold nugget buried beneath the tree outside. How much is it worth?"

She laughed. "My great-great-grandfather never would have missed that. He planted that willow tree to commemorate the college's grand opening."

"Interesting, but this is an economics class and not history. Any other ideas?"

She was driving me crazy. I could tell by the flicker of mischief in her eyes she knew more than she let on.

She shrugged. "Seems irrelevant to me."

I'd had about enough of her disobedience.

I folded my arms across my chest. She made me wish for corporeal punishment to be reinstated. I'd bend her right over my desk and smack the correct answer out of her.

"Well, perhaps you should leave my class and come back once you find it relevant, then?"

"Relax, that's not what I meant. It's irrelevant because until someone digs it up and assigns it a value, it's worthless."

Finally.

I dropped my arms back to my sides. "So, what does that teach us about the basis of the economy?"

She sighed as if nothing pained her more than to be forced into revealing her cleverness. "People, Professor Byrne. That's what you want to hear, right? The foundation of economies are people, not resources."

I smirked at her.

Good girl, was that so hard?

"And what does that give them the power to do?"

"Manipulate resources. Is that all?" she asked.

"It is. Thank you, Ms. Brooks. Manipulation of resource demand and fluctuation in market value..."

I trailed off when I saw she'd picked up her phone once again, feigning disinterest. But I knew she was paying attention to me just as much as I was to her for the rest of the class. So, I let her carry on her ruse of aloofness.

I continued on with my lecture.

Somehow, it made it easier knowing her gaze wasn't fixated on me.

Even if that was what I wanted.

To indulge in her undivided attention and explore whatever joys it would bring.

A flash of memory of her round hips and ass, laced with her skimpy thong as she bent over my desk earlier, haunted me.

Knowing all of that was hiding under her clothing was torturous. Or was it just thinking about how much better her ass would look with a red imprint of my hand on it that was doing me in? She was still wearing the trench coat she'd covered up with earlier. Was her little outfit still concealed beneath?

Fuck me.

I had to stop these fantasies in their tracks or it was going to be a long semester.

Especially if I spent the duration of it fucking her in my head.

When class ended, and the students cleared out, she stayed seated until all the stragglers had disappeared. She continued to feign being absorbed in her phone, even though I was certain she was as aware of my presence as I was of hers.

I leaned against the desk in the lecture hall, watching her. "Did you want to discuss today's lecture?"

She lifted her purse, tucked her phone into it, and looked up at me.

"Yes, don't do that again."

I furrowed my brow and pushed away from my desk to approach hers. "Don't do what again? Encourage you to take part?"

"Put me on the spot like that. I work hard to keep a low profile around here, Professor Byrne, and I won't have you spoiling it for me."

I raised my eyebrows.

Low profile? After today's display, I wasn't buying it.

"My dad—"

I set my palm on her desk with more force than intended and it made a loud slapping noise, which shut her up. "Let me stop you right there."

She sucked in a breath and looked up at me through black-painted lashes, her blue eyes wide.

"I'm well aware of who your daddy is, Ms. Brooks, but make no mistake while you're in my presence." I cleared my throat. "Rather, while you're in my *class,* I expect your full attention and respect from now on. Am I making myself clear?"

A slow smile spread across her face as her eyes dropped to my hand on her desk, my knuckles white from gripping it too hard. I pulled my hand away, and she lifted her purse to her shoulder and stood. "Crystal." She stepped toward me, looking up at me. She may have been only chest high, but I could tell by her expression she felt like a giantess. "You have nothing to worry about, Mr. Byrne. I couldn't ignore you even if I wanted to."

She reached out and dusted her fingertips over my cheek.

I grabbed her by the wrist of the rebellious hand and held it away from me in the space between us.

She sucked in a breath, but there was a flash of something that danced in her eyes and it wasn't fear. My rough touch had impacted her, all right, but there was an unspoken delight that she was failing to conceal. "You had some glitter on your face."

I released her wrist. "I see."

She twisted her wrist and gestured at her face. "I'm a fan of a little sparkle, but I can tell that's not your style, is it, Professor?"

As if she needed to point it out. The subtle sparkle of her lips as she spoke was almost hypnotizing, even without her calling attention to it.

"No, and I'll have to ask you to keep your hands to yourself from now on, Ms. Brooks."

She started walking toward the door before she stopped and turned to face me again.

"It's not my hand that was twitching with need all lecture long." She turned away again but before she stepped through the door she said, "Good luck controlling *that*, Professor."

She opened the door, leaving me alone—almost—she left behind the echoes of her taunt, and the laughter that followed, to keep me company.

Thank you for reading this excerpt from Elle and Finn's story, Miss Education. It's now live on Amazon and Kindle Unlimited!